Lady Airell's Choice

Ladies of Ardena
Book One

Rachel Skatvold
Ps. 23:1-3

RACHEL SKATVOLD

Edited by: Lisa M. Prysock
Proofread by: Joy Davidson
Author Photo: Jennifer Davidson
Cover Design: Erin Dameron-Hill

For more information on Rachel Skatvold, please visit her website: **www.rachelskatvold.com**

Dedication

For Danielle

I'm so proud of the beautiful and talented young lady you are becoming. Keep writing stories and using your talents to shine for the Lord!

Acknowledgements

As always, there are so many people involved in putting a book together and I would like to take a moment to thank them.

First of all, thank you to God for placing this story in my heart. The characters in this story have taught me so much about redemption.

Second, thank you for those who helped with the publication process. I so appreciate the amazing job done by my editor, Lisa M. Prysock, my proofreader and mom, Joy Davidson and Erin Dameron-Hill for the lovely cover art. Also, thanks to my sister, Jenny Davidson for taking my author photo and my uncle, David Webster for your knowledge about genealogy and Ireland.

A big thanks to some special ladies in my reader's group: Susan, Sharon, Linda, Dorothy, Natalya, Merrie, Katie, Patti, Sara. Sarah P., Halita, Sarah T., Michelle, Arletta, Debbie, Denise, Rory, Teri and Carol for participating in my character naming contest. The names you chose are amazing and I loved using them in the story!

Last but not least, thank you to my husband, John, my kids, my extended family and church family for all your love and support. Also, I'd like to give a shout out to my beta readers, reviewers and loyal readers waiting patiently for the next book to come out. You all are such an encouragement and I appreciate you.

Blessings!

Author's Note

Dear Readers,

Thank you for reading the first book in the *Ladies of Ardena Series*! You are about to embark on an epic journey with Lady Airell, Princess of Daireann, filled with adventure, danger, love and faith. However, before you embark on this journey, there are a few things I would like to share with you to make your reading experience more enjoyable.

I have wanted to write a historical novel set in a place similar to Ireland for a while because of my Irish heritage, so I was excited when this story idea materialized. Ardena is not a real place—only a figment of my imagination—but has been inspired by Irish and Scottish culture and history.

To make the story more authentic, there are Irish and Scottish words used for character names, and places throughout the story. If you would like to check pronunciations and meanings for these words, I have included them in the back of the book. There is also a family lineage page to discover the connections between the different kingdoms in Ardena and how the characters are related. It will grow as the series progresses.

Thank you for reading, *Lady Airell's Choice* and I hope you enjoy! Blessings.

Rachel

"The LORD is my shepherd; I shall not want. He maketh me to lie down in green pastures: he leadeth me beside the still waters. He restoreth my soul: he leadeth me in the paths of righteousness for his name's sake." ~ Psalm 23:1-3

Prologue

Kingdom of Daireann, Ardena
Spring, 1187 AD

Lady Airell perched on the highest ridge overlooking Loch Maorga, gazing whimsically at the misty waters below. A light northern wind teased the golden strands of hair around her face as she relaxed onto the soft green bed of undergrowth. Seeing the vibrant sky above and the blooms of lemon buttercups, magenta knapweed and blue-eyed grass surrounding her, the young princess released a contented sigh. It was a rare, clear spring day when the rain held off and allowed the sun to beam down freely. Being here, in her favorite refuge in the entire kingdom, she felt as though God had given her a brief vision of heaven. Could any land be more beautiful and majestic here on earth as her homeland? She couldn't fathom such a thought.

"Airell!" a wispy voice called, nearly carried away by the breeze. "Airell, Father wishes to speak with you."

She propped up on her elbows, glancing at her younger sister as she sat down beside her. "Is it urgent?"

Gwyneth relaxed onto the bed of soft grass, hazel eyes gazing at the cloudless sky above them. She drew in a few deep breaths, winded from the trek up the ridge. "I do not know. He merely requested that I fetch you. He's waiting in the courtyard gardens."

Airell rested back again and pillowed her head in the crook of her elbow, dreading the inevitable conversation awaiting her. "Thank you, Gwyn. I'll go in a few moments. I only wish to enjoy the sun on my face for a little longer."

Gwyneth flipped her long raven braid over one shoulder and grasped her older sister's hand. The smile she tried to suppress sent a foreboding feeling through her. "Do you really think it to be true about Prince Tristan?"

"I do not know what to believe," Airell admitted, drawing in a shaky breath. She still remembered her first meeting with the prince five years ago. He was a handsome young man about her age, with golden hair and calming green eyes. He had been polite and charming in her presence—the portrait of what a young ruler should be. Airell, typically more outgoing than her father liked, had been unusually shy in his presence. Even now, her heart quickened at the mention of his name.

"Oh, I envy you, sister," Gwyneth murmured, bringing Airell out of her daydream. "You are free now—old enough to marry and travel to a new kingdom. 'Twill be such a wonderful adventure."

She turned to her sister who had resumed gazing at the sky. Didn't Gwyn realize the life of a princess was anything *but* free? "Please do not envy me, sister. Enjoy this carefree time of your youth, living in our homeland. Treasure it. Soon enough, you'll have to leave and bid farewell to everyone you love, as I must do."

A small tear formed in the corner of her younger sister's eye. "Yes, I know you are right. Forgive me."

Airell squeezed her sister's hand, hoping she hadn't been too harsh. "There is nothing to forgive, *Devin.*"

Her sister smiled at the term of endearment meaning, *little deer.* It was a name only used by her elder sister. "We better go. Father will scold me if we wait too much longer."

Airell chuckled. "Aye, but you are father's favorite, Gwyn. He won't be too hard on you. In fact, he'll most likely blame me." She sat up and plucked a few blades of grass from her hair.

Her sister grinned with bright hazel eyes and sat up with her, pausing to pick a small periwinkle blossom and tuck it behind her elder sister's ear. "I'll race you to the courtyard." Before Airell had a chance to reply, her sister gathered her skirts and dashed off down the craggy hill.

She scoffed playfully and bounded down the hill after her. "Distract me with a flower, aye?" she called. Her sister's jovial laughter carried on the wind as her raven braid bounced behind her head, but soon she caught up and their laughter blended together like a cheerful springtime song.

When they reached the gardens, both girls had to stop with their hands braced against their thighs to catch their breath.

Gwyneth patted her shoulder. "'Twas a tie."

"Aye," Airell agreed, still struggling to breathe through her laughter.

After parting ways with her sister, she journeyed

around the fountain in the courtyard bordered with yellow buttercups and then meandered down one of the garden paths, until reaching the rose bushes—her father's favorite place in the garden. An elderly gardener smiled while tending the bushes and gave a slight bow before snipping a white bloom off and presenting it to her. She lifted the flower and inhaled its heavenly fragrance. Then she smiled and thanked the gardener before navigating the bend in the path. There she found her father, talking with her brother, Arlan. They could have been a painted mural on one of the palace walls—hands clasped behind their backs and facing Beatha Valley below the courtyard. They were muscular, tall and bearded, with their golden shoulder-length hair halfway clipped back with small silver clasps.

A moment later, her father patted Arlan's shoulder and her brother turned to walk away. When he saw her standing behind them, he tried to hide the discouraged look in his blue eyes, but Airell knew him too well. The winds of change were coming. She could sense it.

"See you at dinner, Sister," Arlan murmured, pausing to grasp her shoulder before he walked away.

Her father, King Fallon, remained with his back toward her, his royal blue robe bordered with silver fur blowing in the breeze. "Come speak with me for a moment, my precious daughter."

Airell placed the white rose aside, hands trembling as her fingers curled around the ledge of the stone wall.

Her father gazed out over Beatha Valley with the gardens, vineyards and village in the distance. "Your great grandfather loved this valley. Now its success has far surpassed any dreams he envisioned. God has truly blessed this kingdom with peace and prosperity."

"Aye, He has, and this kingdom is blessed to have

you as king, too." Airell's heart filled with love for her father as she linked her arm with his and rested her head against his strong shoulder. He was a gentle, kind and fair ruler, who always put the needs of his family and kingdom above his own.

He patted her arm with his free hand. "And I am blessed to have a daughter like you."

She smiled and released him. "So what did you want to speak to me about?"

Her father looked her in the eyes for the first time, his expression troubled. "King Malcolm has been showing signs of aggression toward the other king-doms—pillaging and burning small villages in the north." Airell gasped, remembering rumors about the Dark Lord of Brannagh. He succeeded to the throne as a regent for his nephew several years before, but seemed in no hurry to give up his place of authority. Hearing his name made her tremble, however, her father continued on in spite of her emotions. "There will be a meeting in Órlaith soon to discuss how we will work together to keep the peace."

Airell's heart dropped. "So you'll be leaving?"

"Aye. Two days from now."

Two days. She didn't know why, but the words struck fear within her heart. Her father had departed on many journeys in her eighteen years of life and had always come back unharmed, but this time felt different. "Your brother will be helping your mother rule in my stead and I will be counting on you to help them."

"I will," she agreed with a nod, finally understanding her brother's melancholy behavior. He wanted to go along, but his request had been denied.

"Now, we have more important matters to discuss." He smiled and placed his hands on her shoulders, letting out a deep sigh. She noticed his cobalt eyes looked tired and the streaks of silver in his blond hair and beard seemed more prominent than usual. "Since you've come of age, I've received letters from a few dukes and even King Ewan from the northwest mountain kingdom, seeking your hand in marriage."

Airell shuddered and her eyes grew wide. "King Ewan?" She had never met him personally, but had heard people talk about the handsome, dark-haired ruler with mysterious, steel blue eyes from North Rhona. He was almost ten years her elder, but that wasn't what bothered her. Age difference didn't matter much in their culture. According to her sister-in-law, Lady Reagan, he was a wise and kind ruler. However, he lived high in the mountains, known for their treacherous, wild terrain and savagely cold winters. She couldn't imagine living in such a harsh, unforgiving land.

Her father didn't react to her discomfort, but continued on. "Oh and one more...Prince Tristan from the Kingdom of Órlaith."

There was the name at the end—the one that made her heart quicken. Prince Tristan—from what their people called *The Golden Kingdom*—sought her hand in marriage. Airell looked down and drew in a shaky breath. "Is that all?" Her voice held a bit of humor to mask her apprehension. "Have you and mother chosen one of them yet?"

Her father let out the deep, regal laugh she loved hearing before turning serious and lifting her chin with his index finger until their eyes met again. "'Tis not our decision to make."

She stared at him in surprise. "'Tis not? You arranged Arlan's betrothal to Lady Reagan in advance when he was nine years of age. I always believed it was my duty to make a good alliance for the kingdom."

"'Twas different for Arlan, being the firstborn and Lady Reagan's kingdom needed protection in exchange for gold from the mountains of Rhona. Your brother knew an arranged marriage would be necessary for the future king. They grew to love to love each other in time, but I want something different for my daughters."

Airell bit her lip, finally understanding her father's words. "I may choose?"

He nodded. "Aye."

A massive weight lifted off her shoulders at her father's words. "Thank you!" Airell hugged him, unable to contain her excitement.

He laughed when she released him. "Now, we will have a feast to celebrate my departure. Your mother will need help planning for the occasion."

"As you wish, Father." She kissed his cheek and then danced out of the courtyard as if on a cloud. *I may choose*, her heart sang all the way into the castle. *I may choose!* She had never felt so free in all her life.

The feast had been a merry time of celebration for the entire kingdom, but now it was time to say farewell to her father and the rest of his company leaving for Órlaith.

Airell fought tears while watching her father and mother in the courtyard. She was certain they had shared a goodbye kiss in privacy, but now they simply stood facing each other. Her father leaned his forehead against hers and closed his eyes while smoothing his fingers over her long raven hair. "Mo shíorghrá," he whispered, which she knew meant, *my eternal love*. Her mother whispered something back, but Airell couldn't quite hear it.

She turned away to hide the tears rolling down her cheeks. Would she ever be blessed enough to find a love like her parents had? They were rulers of an entire kingdom, yet still made time to share their deepest feelings with each other. It was a scary thought, transitioning to the next stage in her adult life—to marry and then move to her husband's kingdom—but she wanted to experience the kind of love her parents had found. Now she knew what she had to do.

After embracing his queen one last time, the king went down the line, bidding farewell to her elder brother, Arlan, then Airell and Gwyneth last. He turned to go before Airell finally gathered enough courage to ask him. "Father!" she blurted out, running to him.

He turned with misty eyes and forced a sad smile. "Yes, my daughter?"

She fumbled over her words as she whispered them for his ears only. "While...while you are in Órlaith, will you inform Prince Tristan I will accept his proposal of marriage?"

Her father's smile of approval sent a crimson hue blooming over her cheeks. "Fine choice. I will do as you wish."

They shared one last embrace and then, with a swish of his royal blue robe, her father and the rest of his company left the courtyard. She watched from above with the rest of the royal family as he mounted his horse and rode through Beatha Valley toward the road. From there, it would be a two-day journey to the harbor, then a week journey by sea. She prayed for his safety and theirs during his month-long absence. After all, she knew too well the unexpected dangers of traveling by sea.

Airell pushed her apprehensive thoughts away and instead waved to her father before he faded from view. She would think of his return in the summer. There would be an even greater celebration then—and hopefully a young prince accompanying him. Aye, there were plenty of things to look forward to and dream about in her future, of that she was certain.

CHAPTER ONE

Changing Winds

The sound of chiming bells awoke Airell from her sleep—a joyous sound she used to love hearing in the morning. It usually signified some kind of celebration and today was no different. She covered her yawn and stretched as her maids flurried into the room to help her dress. Their lighthearted chatter lifted her mood for a moment, but then the heaviness returned as she crossed the room to look out her window. The leaves had started to fall, painting the courtyard and nearby hills in vibrant shades of crimson, russet brown and burnt orange. She loved the fall. If only her heart didn't feel so numb.

"We must hurry, Your Majesty," Merrie urged. "The ceremony starts in an hour! You mustn't be late."

"Aye," she agreed and allowed them to help her dress. As they slipped her favorite red gown over her head, she stared at the wall, eyes vacant. It felt odd to not be wearing mourning clothes. Shouldn't the kingdom cry for their fallen ruler longer than only a few months? It seemed wrong.

Airell's thoughts traveled back to the tragic day a few haggard members of the king's guard returned to Daireann with her father's body. King Malcolm had conquered Órlaith shortly after their arrival. The entire Órlaithan Royal Family was presumed dead as well, including Prince Tristan—adding salt to the deep wound in her heart. In one moment, Airell's entire life had shifted on the breeze. She no longer recognized the path ahead of her.

The door creaked, opening and closing behind her. Then her mother's voice invaded her scattered thoughts. "Airell, we have to be strong today. Your brother needs our support."

She nodded, but remained silent—torn between her duties as Princess of Daireann and the raw emotions welling up inside.

Her mother's slender fingers picked up where Airell's maids had left off and began tightening the strings on the back of her gown. "Above all, your father longed to keep his family and kingdom safe. He always put his own feelings and safety last. Now today, we must do the same, even though it pains us."

She blinked away a few tears and turned to her mother, noticing the dark circles under her eyes. "What if I cannot do it?"

Her mother reached to tuck a loose golden curl behind Airell's ear. "We will get through this day together...hand in hand, my daughter."

During the coronation, Airell managed to find a deep calm within her soul by remembering a favorite chapter from the Bible kept in the chapel. It was in Latin, but being well educated in languages, she had an advantage over most living in the kingdom. They had to rely on a priest to translate. She felt thankful that God used the twenty-third Psalm to comfort her now.

"The LORD is my shepherd; I shall not want.

He maketh me to lie down in green pastures: he leadeth me beside the still waters.

He restoreth my soul: he leadeth me in the paths of righteousness for his name's sake."

Christianity had only come to their lands during her great-grandfather's reign, yet her father had told her stories of how much had changed in their kingdom since then and how much they had prospered.

Airell smiled to herself, remembering her father, King Fallon, now walked beside *The Great Shepherd*, in heaven.

Gwyneth squeezed her hand, bringing Airell back to the present. Her sister smiled and gave her a silent look, reminding her an important part of the ceremony approached.

She smiled back, amazed her younger sister managed to stay so calm in the past months. Out of the three siblings, she had been the strongest, much like their father. Sometimes it seemed as though he stared out at her from Gwyneth's eyes. Then, Airell knew she could be strong, too, for her father's blood also ran through her veins.

A moment later, the musicians began playing, chasing away every hint of leftover gloom within her. Then she watched as Arlan and his wife, Reagan, came down the walkway together to be crowned King and Queen of Daireann. Her sister-in-law's flowing emerald gown looked stunning, bringing out her long auburn curls. Her brother's robe was dark green as well, showing their solidarity with one another. They would rule over two kingdoms now, as one mind and one heart.

As the priest placed the crown on Arlan's head and handed him the scepter, a warm feeling spread through Airell's heart. Her brother was young—only twenty-one years of age, yet she knew he would be a kind, fair and gentle king, like their father had been. He would put their kingdom first—making sacrifices for the good of the people. At that moment, Airell also knew something about herself. With her father gone, along with the peace they had enjoyed for years, the winds had changed. She would have to make sacrifices for her family and her kingdom. No more would she dream of having choices and being free. Serving her kingdom was her duty as Princess Airell of Daireann.

Airell sat straight up in bed and her eyes darted around the dark room. Only a thin stream of moonlight filtered through the window. What had awakened her? Then she heard it—the beating of distant drums and a deep blast from a horn. A chill ran up Airell's spine while snatching a robe from a nearby chair. While tying it around her waist, she rushed out her chamber door and down the long hallway with haste, nearly running headlong into her younger sister coming from the other direction.

Gwyneth's frightened doe eyes searched hers in the dim light. "Airell, what is going on?"

She pulled her sister close, providing comfort for both of them and stammered, "I...I'm not certain yet. Gwyn, you need to return to your chambers. Lock the door and do not come out until I come for you."

Gwyneth shook her head and clung to her older sister even tighter. "No, please don't leave me alone. I wish to stay with you."

Airell agreed reluctantly and held her sister close as they made their way out to the ramparts overlooking the valley. What she saw made her blood run cold. The nearby village and crops were on fire, filling the horizon with an ominous red glow. Then she saw the massive army marching toward the castle. They were under attack.

CHAPTER TWO

The Siege

Lady Reagan clung to her husband's arm while they peered over the edge of the terrace outside the royal chambers. Her heart rumbled in fear with each ominous drum beat. Meeting Arlan's troubled gaze only intensified it. Even in the dim moonlight, Reagan saw the dark circles under his cobalt eyes. He hadn't been sleeping or eating right since his father's death. So much responsibility had been thrust upon his shoulders in a short amount of time—and now a siege from an unknown enemy. It was all too much and too fast for him to gain his bearings.

Reagan pushed her own fear aside and drew strength from deep within. She couldn't remember a time in her life when she *hadn't* been a queen—first to her kingdom, South Rhona, at five years old after the death of her father—and as of yesterday, she had become Queen Consort of Daireann. Her husband and both of their countries needed her to be strong.

She faced Arlan and took both his large hands in

hers. "Now is the time for courage, my love. Our people are relying on us to defend them."

All at once, the apprehension in his eyes faded and the courageous leader she knew and loved returned. He gave her a fragile smile that gradually grew strong and confident. "Aye, thank you for your wisdom, my queen. What would I do without you by my side?" He pulled her into his arms, weaving his hands through her auburn hair while kissing her with such a tender passion she never wanted to let him go. Then he headed back into their chambers, pulling her with him. "If it is King Malcolm of Brannagh, he'll be relentless. He will not show mercy to even the women and children inside this fortress."

Reagan gulped as they crossed to his suit of armor in the corner of the room. "I know. 'Tis why we must stand strong to protect it. If a peace treaty cannot be made, we must fight with all we have. But there has to be something he wants. I know he has a ravenous lust for gold."

Arlan nodded while donning his chainmail and chest plate. Then he turned so Reagan could tighten the straps. "Aye, he wants gold...and something else I'm not willing to part with."

Her eyes widened while helping him strap more armor on. "What is it?"

His eyes looked troubled again for only a moment before he shook his head and managed a smile. "You needn't worry about it, my love. 'Twill not come to that. I'll collaborate with my uncle and order our archers to take their place on the ramparts. Then he will make sure our foot soldiers and cavalry will be ready as well. Lives will be lost tonight, but we will be victorious by the morning sunrise. I'm certain of it."

Reagan cringed. There wasn't a single memory from her childhood in South Rhona that wasn't tinged by the effects of civil war. After fleeing from several conquered fortresses, her mother finally made the decision to accept a marriage alliance with Daireann. At twelve years old, she came to live in Arlan's kingdom until they married six years later. Now the land she had grown to think of as home would be ravaged by war, too. The thought tormented her.

Shaking free of her worried thoughts, Lady Reagan became aware that Arlan was fully armored and ready for battle. She embraced him one last time and then walked with him to their chamber door.

He cupped her cheek in his hand and his cobalt eyes grew intense. "I want you to promise me something. Find my mother and sisters. Then, hide in the secret passageways beneath the castle until this is all over. Do not leave, no matter what happens."

Reagan bit her lip, knowing she couldn't lie to her husband, even if it would make him feel better. "'Tis not in my blood to hide, Arlan."

His pleading look of despair broke her heart. "Please? I will not be able to think clearly if I know you and the rest of my family are in danger."

She let out a sigh of resignation. "I promise to lead your family to the hidden passageways, but I cannot promise to stay with them. I will be safe in the infirmary, tending to the wounded if I am needed. 'Tis one of the safest places in the castle, strongly reinforced and close to the underground entrance."

"*Reagan*..." he scolded gently. You know how I feel about you working down there. 'Tis no place for a lady, not to mention, a *queen*."

She grinned up at him innocently, pleading with her

eyes for him to give in. "Perhaps I'll be the one who rewrites the definition of a queen."

A reluctant chuckle slipped from his mouth. "Leave it to you to rewrite the rulebooks a day after ascending to the Daireann throne. These people do not know what they have gotten themselves into."

She laughed with him for a moment and then turned serious, gently stroking his cheek with her fingertips. "Arlan, I cannot sit by and do nothing. I must help our people."

Arlan's worried look turned to admiration at her declaration of loyalty to Daireann's citizens. "*Our people,*" he repeated with a regal grin. "Yes, I realize now more than ever, *our people* are blessed to have you as their queen—as am I, my Rhona bride."

He kissed her forehead, lingering to hold her for a moment longer. Then in an instant, he was gone.

Lady Airell's breath caught in her throat as she held her sister. They both watched with wide eyes as the archers showered the vast army approaching the castle with arrows. Many on the front lines fell, but it barely made a dent in their numbers. As the sun began to rise over the horizon, she observed the massive scale of their army. It stretched out over the valley in never-ending rows. When the front lines had fallen, the next row would take their place. Then, when the archer's arrows were spent, she heard her uncle, the Duke of Beatha, call for the cavalry and foot soldiers.

Rallying to protect their kingdom, they rushed out with brave battle cries. She watched her brother and uncle upon their horses, the distant fire gleaming off their armor. Her brother had never looked more brave and fierce as a king, yet her heart lurched, fearing for his safety.

At first, their lines seemed to break through the rows of shadow-like soldiers below. However, before long, her heart sunk, seeing all the fallen warriors on the battlefield. The Daireann army was no match for Brannagh's.

Someone came up from behind and pulled them away. "Don't watch." Her mother whispered, holding them close.

Airell covered her mouth and wept in horror and grief as they retreated into the safety of the castle. Why wouldn't Arlan try to make a peace treaty? It seemed irrational to try and fight when the enemy had the advantage of surprise and numbers.

A few minutes later, Lady Reagan rushed toward them, accompanied by four guards. Her red curls flowed behind her like a glowing flame before stopping in front of them. "Oh, I've been searching everywhere!" She leaned over and braced herself against the castle wall, trying to catch her breath. "Arlan sent me to find you. He wishes for all of you to hide in the secret passages."

A few minutes later, they had journeyed to the lower levels of the castle. Airell and Reagan felt along the wall for the hidden door. Finally, Airell felt a portion of the wall give way and a small, dark passage opened before them. The guards lit torches and guided the royal family through the winding pathways. Cobwebs stuck to Airell's hair as they walked and the sound of dripping water filled her eardrums. Finally they entered a small chamber with stone benches along the wall, scrolls on shelves and a large locked trunk. In the corner sat a desk and chair with velvet upholstery.

"What is this place?" Airell asked in wonder.

"The king's secret meeting room, Milady," one of the guards replied. "You will be safe here."

Lady Reagan nodded. "This is where the king wanted you to stay. I'll come and let you know when it is safe to return."

Airell's mouth hinged open. "Where are you going?"

The young queen pursed her lips, seeming reluctant to tell her. Finally she looked up and her eyes clouded over. "I'm going to help in the infirmary. 'Tis not in my blood to hide."

She took her sister-in-law's hand and nodded in understanding. "Nor is it in mine. I shall go with you."

"Airell, no," her mother protested, eyes filled with terror. "Please, stay with us."

She turned to her mother with a gentle, knowing smile. "I *need* to do this. These are our people and they're dying to protect us. I have to try and help them. I'll be careful and if I hear of any danger within the castle, I will return with haste."

Her mother nodded and held her close for a moment. "Take two of the king's guards. I love you."

"Love you, too," she murmured, trying to keep her wits about her.

Then after saying an emotional farewell to Gwyneth, she followed Lady Reagan and the guards back up the passage. Airell didn't know what she would find in the infirmary or what dangers they would face if the enemy made it into the castle, but she did know one thing. Years from now, when people told stories about the Siege on the Kingdom of Daireann, she wanted to be known as the princess who fought for her people—not the one who hid.

CHAPTER THREE

Secrets

As Airell followed her sister-in-law into the infirmary, she was nearly blown over by the stench of blood, sweat and death. She paused in the doorway to cover her nose with the hem of her robe, but nausea swept over her regardless. The sight of the room overflowing with injured and dying warriors pushed a sob into her throat. The previous night they had all been feasting and celebrating with their families after her brother's coronation. Now they were dying in anguish or barely clinging to life. Airell fought the urge to flee from the room and hide with her mother and sister.

Through her fog, she heard Reagan calling for her and gathered enough courage to enter the room. She found the young queen kneeling next to a soldier with a gash in his leg. "W-what can I do to h-help?

Reagan handed her a long strip of white bandage. "Here, will you put pressure on the wound while I gather my supplies?"

Airell ignored the queasy feeling in her stomach and

nodded, concentrating on their patient. He was young—about her age, maybe even younger—with his entire life ahead of him, only hours before. She had to put her own feelings aside to help him. Airell doubled the bandage over several times and then placed it over the wound, applying pressure, like Reagan instructed. The young man groaned in pain as she tried to stay calm herself. She felt so helpless, unable to comfort him.

Reagan saved her, talking in a low, calming voice and asking his name. When he told her it was Liam, she assured him he was going to live and he was very brave. Airell watched her sister-in-law in amazement. How did she manage to stay so calm? She recalled seeing the queen go into the infirmary frequently to visit patients—mostly children who had fallen ill or had minor injuries. Airell thought she simply liked to be with the children, since she hadn't any of her own yet. However, now she saw her sister-in-law possessed quite a gift for soothing and tending to patients.

Airell held Liam's hand while Reagan cleaned and stitched his wound. Then, when he was bandaged and resting comfortably, they moved on to the next patient. To her relief, the physician and his assistants took on the more serious injuries.

Time blurred together, but as the day wore on, Airell started to relax and actually talk to the injured men while her sister-in-law worked. Eventually Reagan even taught her how to clean and stitch wounds under her supervision.

At a lull in the madness, she turned to Reagan in curiosity. "Where did you learn so much about caring for the injured?"

Reagan sighed and washed her hands in a nearby

water basin. "My mother. She was what my people call a healer. When my father was a young man, he became injured in a hunting accident. She came across him in the woods and took him back to her hut. She nursed him back to health and they fell in love. The kingdom was outraged that the king had married a commoner, but eventually my mother won them over. She has such a charming way about her." Reagan smiled. "Anyway, she taught me everything she knew about healing from an early age. I enjoy helping people, even though it's not *proper* for a queen, as Arlan would say."

They both chuckled in spite of the tense atmosphere in the infirmary and then sobered, hearing commotion and loud footsteps in the hallway. Reagan gripped the small dagger hanging from her belt and Airell followed suit.

Then a moment later, the voices became clear and everything went quiet in the room. "Make way...we need a physician! The king has been injured!"

The color left Lady Reagan's cheeks as several of the king's guards carried her husband into the infirmary with an arrow protruding from his left side. It was lodged in the one tiny gap in his armor that allowed his arms to move freely.

"Arlan!" she cried out, rushing to her husband's side. She took his hand and kissed it, soaking it with her tears in the process. "You're going to be all right, my love. Can you hear me?" He looked in her direction but couldn't seem to focus. His breathing came in shallow gasps.

One of the guards lowered his head and bowed before her. "I apologize, Your Majesty. None of us even saw the arrow coming."

After a moment Reagan calmed herself and started thinking like a nurse again. She studied his wound, letting out a sigh of relief, before turning to Airell who stood close behind. "His injury looks severe, but does not appear to have pierced his heart. 'Tis good news."

Her sister-in-law nodded, but looked so pale and distraught, Reagan wondered if she even understood her words.

The physician rushed over, wiping his hands with a towel while speaking to the guards. "Take His Majesty to my personal chambers. He will be safer there and have some privacy."

Reagan followed the guards as they carried Arlan down the hallway to the physician's chambers and laid him on the bed. She stayed with her husband, but noticed Airell hadn't followed them. She must have remained in the hallway.

She helped remove her husband's armor, careful to be gentle and then watched closely as the physician examined Arlan's wound. "I fear the arrow may have pierced one of his lungs, but if we work quickly he should recover."

She nodded and watched him cross the room and start grinding up some herbs to make him sleep. However, when he returned with the cup, Arlan's eyes became alert and he refused to drink.

"R...Reagan?" he rasped instead, turning his head toward her.

She took the cup of medicine from the physician and knelt by her husband's side—kissing his hand and willing his strength to return. "I'm here, my love. You're going to overcome this, but you must drink this medicine and allow the physician to remove the arrow."

He coughed, wincing with the effort and continued his labored breathing. Every word seemed to tax his strength. "We have to...keep...fighting. You will have to be regent...in my stead."

She nodded and shushed him, pausing to smooth a few blond tangles off his forehead. "Please, try not to talk, my love. I will think of some way to keep everyone safe. Your sister's here, too. She will help me."

"Airell?" His face looked panicked all of a sudden and he tried to sit up.

Reagan struggled to hold down her muscular husband, even in his weakened state. "'Tis all right. She's safe. We both are."

He rested against his pillow again, groaning and breathing erratically. "No...you don't...you don't understand. She...she's more...in danger...than anyone."

Reagan stared at her husband, confused thoughts tangling in her mind. "Arlan, what have you been keeping from me?"

Airell paced outside the physician's chambers, anxious to receive word about her brother's condition. She had wanted to give her sister-in-law a few minutes of privacy with him, but now her heart pulsed with worry.

A few moments later, a guard came to the door, his expression grim. "The king wishes to speak with you, Your Majesty."

She rushed into the room and saw Reagan helping Arlan rest his head back on a pillow after drinking something from a cup. He coughed with a grimace, but then appeared to relax. Airell noticed the doctor in the corner of the room, preparing medical instruments to remove the arrow.

Airell's sister-in-law glanced in her direction with a strained smile. "The medication the physician has prepared is going to make him sleep soon, but you should have a few minutes to talk. I'll give you privacy." She kissed Arlan's cheek and then headed for the far corner of the room to wait.

"Thank you," she murmured as Reagan passed by. Then she sat on a small stool pulled up beside her brother's bed. His face seemed more relaxed now and his breathing more even than when the guards first brought him into the infirmary.

"Sister..." he whispered with a weak smile of relief. "You're safe."

"Aye, I'm safe." She took his hand in hers—surprised at how cold and clammy it felt. Airell knew it had to be from blood loss. "You must stay strong, Arlan. The people of Daireann need you. *I* need you."

He nodded slowly and his eyelids fluttered for a moment, telling Airell the medicine had begun to work. They had limited time to speak. "And I need you to stay out of harm. You must hide in the secret passage with Mother and Gwyneth."

She shook her head. "Reagan and I both decided we will not hide when our people need us."

"*Airell*," he reprimanded in a weak voice. "I wish...you would listen to reason...but I suppose you would think differently...if you knew..." Arlan's voice trailed off and his eyes closed.

"If I knew what?" Airell shook him gently and he stirred. "Please tell me. I need to know."

Arlan's eyelids fluttered again, like staying awake was an impossible task. "Father didn't tell you...and I promised...to keep it secret..."

"What?" Her eyes were wide now, pleading for him to tell her.

"The suitors asking for your hand...there was one more...one he didn't mention...because he forbade it."

Airell's heart thundered so loud in her ears, she could barely hear her brother's waning voice. "Who was he?"

Arlan's face went slack and his voice became so quiet, she had to lean her ear close to his face as he whispered the name. "King...Malcolm."

CHAPTER FOUR

The Choice

Airell left the physician's quarters in a daze and sunk to the floor outside the door, replaying her brother's words in her mind. King Malcolm wanted her to be his queen—the same man whose army was outside their walls—the same man who caused her father's death.

A gasp caught in her throat, realizing this was not a coincidence. Her father had refused the King of Brannagh and he wasn't used to not having his way. All of this was because of her. Airell's father must have gone to Órlaith to talk with the other kingdoms about the tension with King Malcolm, but it was too late.

While Airell sat, rumors of a lull in the battle spread. King Malcolm had pulled back his forces and set up camp in Beatha Valley, giving them time to help more of the wounded. Soon the rumors were confirmed when injured soldiers on cots began to fill up the hallway around her, but now she could not bear to look at them.

It's because of me. This is all because of me.

Her sister-in-law came out of the physician's chambers a while later, looking disheveled but relieved. "The surgery went well. The king is resting comfortably now."

"Oh, good." Airell came out of her fog and stood with Reagan. "May I see him?"

Reagan gripped her arm gently and managed a weak smile. "Aye, Arlan will want to see you when he awakens. I am going to meet with your uncle to discuss the status of our army since I will be acting as regent while the king recovers. I will return soon."

Airell nodded. "Be careful."

Her sister-in-law nodded before departing.

She drew in a deep breath, gathering courage before entering the door behind her. Relief filled her, noticing Arlan breathed easier than before. He still looked pale, but slept peacefully.

Airell sat on the wooden stool next to her brother's bed and gripped his hand. "You're going to survive this, Arlan...and so is our kingdom." She sat for a few moments in silence, watching the slow rise and fall of her brother's chest under the bandages and blankets.

He reminded her so much of their father and had the potential to become a great king, if given the time to grow into the role. Thankfully he had an experienced queen ruling by his side. Reagan was three years his elder and had more wisdom than her years. Airell had confidence her sister-in-law would make a suitable regent while Arlan recovered.

Then she remembered the army camped in the valley and a hopeless feeling returned to her heart. What were they to do? If only they could make some kind of peace treaty.

All at once, Airell gasped as a solution came to her.

The future of Daireann rested on her shoulders—and it all led up to one choice—a choice only she could make.

She leaned down and planted a light kiss on her brother's forehead. "Farewell, Arlan. I will not be here when you awaken. We may never meet again, but I hope you know what I am about to do is to save our kingdom. I hope you'll find it in your heart to forgive me for my choice."

Lady Reagan stood in the armory dressed for battle with a bow in hand and a quiver of arrows slung behind her back. After setting up a target at the far end of the room, she stepped back to the other side and strung her arrow on the bow, poised to release. Her talk with the Duke of Beatha left her much to think about and practicing archery calmed her nerves.

Even though King Malcolm's army had fallen back for the time being and made camp in the valley. Many of Daireann's soldiers were injured and they were running out of options to protect the fortress. If it came to it, she would not hide in the shadows. She would fight for her husband's kingdom until her last breath.

Reagan loosed an arrow and watched as the tip pierced through the target a few inches from the center. *Not good enough.* She tried again, this time landing a little closer. Finally loosing the third arrow, it struck directly in the center and a pleased smile spread across her face.

Arlan had never agreed with her desire to fight in battle and it was something they argued over often. She knew he only longed to protect her. However, Rhona's culture was much different than Darieann's, training women to fight along with the men. She had learned how to use a bow at an early age to defend herself.

Now it could prove useful. She had limited experience wielding a sword, but at least she had a bow, arrows and a small dagger hidden near her belt for protection.

"Your Majesty!"

The sound of Uncle Edmund's voice tore through her thoughts as he entered the armory. Reagan turned to him with wide eyes. "What is it?"

He gave a quick bow and sucked in a quick breath, obviously winded from rushing to find her. "There are three riders headed out across the valley with a white flag of truce."

Now Reagan's emerald eyes flashed, her fiery temper revealing itself for a moment. "What foolish soldiers would do such a thing? If they survive, I'll throw them in the dungeon myself!"

"Your Highness, the riders are not soldiers. Two are the king's own guards and the one in the center has her head covered with a hood and appears to be a noblewoman."

CHAPTER FIVE

Betrothed

Airell's hand trembled as she held the reigns of her horse and urged him forward through the crowd of soldiers. The two guards accompanying her provided some comfort, but the enemy soldiers still terrified her.

They cackled and sneered in her direction, calling out vulgarities she tried to block out by pulling the hood of her cloak a little closer to her face. Airell's mind raced with the repercussions of her decision. While she hoped her status as a princess would protect her, there was no way to know if King Malcolm demanded his men live by a code, or if they simply did as they pleased.

Airell could only pray as she approached the tents and a tall blond soldier with a scarred face approached. "What business do you have here?"

The man's gruff tone almost made her lose her resolve, but she gulped down her fear and raised her chin high. "I am Princess Airell, the daughter of King Fallon. I come under a white flag of truce and wish to discuss my terms with King Malcolm."

The soldier before her let out a sardonic chuckle. "Your terms?"

Her eyes narrowed, faking confidence. "Aye, my terms."

"Very well, come with me," he said. After helping her dismount the horse and ordering her guards to stay outside, he lead her into a large tent with two menacing guards in black armor standing watch outside. Airell took in the scene with wide blue eyes. A large platform sat at the back of the tent, covered with furs and atop them sat two velvet embroidered thrones with one lower than the other. Two tables sat on one side of the tent—one filled with a variety of food and wine. The other was covered with maps.

Several men stood in the tent—about four more guards, a few servants and then two armored men in the center of the space, leaning over the second table and looking deep in discussion. One was tall and muscular with a dark bushy beard and eyebrows and a bald head underneath his jeweled crown. The other was much younger—tall and lean with more streamlined armor and shoulder-length chestnut brown hair. He would have been handsome, if not for the deep scowl on his face.

The first man stood to his full height and his dark eyes squinted at her in the dim light. "What is the meaning of this, Lord Caerul?" he snarled, turning to the soldier who had led her in. "You would bring a strange woman into my tent with no warning or introduction?"

The tall man visibly bristled at the king's anger. "I apologize, Your Majesty. This is Lady Airell, Princess of Daireann. She has come under a white flag of truce."

He bowed and left the tent.

Airell took his words as a cue to drop her dark hood and curtsy before the king.

A crooked grin snaked across his face. "Well, this is a pleasant surprise indeed. Welcome, Your Majesty." He then turned to his guards and flicked his hand in the direction of the tent entrance. "Leave us."

Airell watched as they obeyed instantly, leaving her alone with only King Malcolm and the younger man who refused to meet her gaze.

With a swish of his crimson robe, the king settled onto the higher throne and the younger man settled on the lower one, glaring down at the furs beneath his feet.

King Malcolm stared down at Airell, studying her with calculating dark eyes. "You are as fair as the rumors say. I understand why King Fallon wished to hide you away."

Lady Airell blushed at his comment, suddenly desiring to have a homely appearance. He stared at her with hungry eyes, like she was a trophy to be won—a status symbol—not a princess or even a lady. Anger suddenly boiled up within her, remembering this man had caused her father's death. However, she gulped down her nerves and went on with her plan, even though everything within her screamed otherwise. "King Malcolm, I am willing to make a treaty with you in order to keep my kingdom from destruction."

His eyebrow lifted. "I'm listening."

She drew in a ragged breath. "I understand you requested my hand in marriage, but my father refused. This decision was made without my knowledge. I would like to remedy the situation, in exchange for peace between our kingdoms." She went on, suggesting a generous dowry and the resources they would be willing to trade in order to have peace.

To Airell's dismay, King Malcolm stopped listening to her. Instead he engaged in a heated discussion with the young man beside him, speaking too low for her to hear. When they were done a few minutes later, the king looked up at her with a victorious grin. "I accept your treaty...with a few amendments, of course."

Airell shifted uncomfortably on her feet. "Amendments?"

"Aye," the king said and with a flourish of his robes, he stood and began to pace on the platform with his hands clutched behind his back. "Your father misunderstood my request of marriage. Sadly, I already have a queen. 'Tis a shame to turn down a beautiful woman like yourself, but unfortunately I am a very loyal man."

Airell frowned. "I'm afraid I don't understand."

He stopped pacing and stood next to the young man on the platform, patting his shoulder. "I intended for you to be betrothed to my nephew, Prince Tiernay."

Her heart raced as the prince met her gaze. His eyes were a pleasing shade of hazel, but cold as ice and his handsome face distorted with a fierce look of displeasure and some other emotion she couldn't quite place. Airell didn't know who intimidated her more—King Malcolm or Prince Tiernay. They were both terrifying in their own way. Yet, she had no choice. "Very well," she agreed barely above a whisper, fearing she'd just signed her life away to a monster.

Lady Reagan's auburn curls blew back in the breeze while watching King Malcolm's army retreat into the distance. In their wake they left fire, destruction and death. Reagan should have been glad to see them go, yet the letter in her hand only brought more despair.

She shielded her eyes from the late afternoon sun, making out a hooded woman on a horse. She looked back once, paused and then turned to go with the rest of the soldiers. Reagan's heart lurched, watching her go. Airell had proven to be braver than anyone in the kingdom. She had signed away her freedom to buy them peace—but what a costly peace it had been. Reagan couldn't imagine what it would be like not seeing her around the castle or what horrors Airell would face in her new life.

She had been shocked when the guards returned without her, explaining the princess had agreed to marry the Prince of Brannagh in exchange for peace. They hadn't even allowed her the privilege of saying goodbye. The guards had been ordered to gather Lady Airell's belongings, along with the gold and gems they had agreed upon for a dowry. Now she was leaving them forever. How would she explain this to Arlan or his family?

Lady Reagan unfolded the letter one more time with tears clouding her eyes, hoping to glean some kind of comfort from her sister-in-law's words.

My beloved family,

I write to inform you I have agreed to marry Prince Tiernay of the northern kingdom. I was not forced to make this decision, but made it of my own free will, in order to make peace between our two nations. Please, do not weep for my sake. I hope to find happiness in this new life in a new land. Father told me before his death that I could choose a suitor and therefore I have chosen a match that will benefit our kingdom. My one regret is not being able to bid you all a proper farewell. Please know I love you all

Rachel Skatvold

and will be thinking of and praying for you often, hoping one day we will meet again.

Sincerely yours,
Airell

CHAPTER SIX

The Voyage

The two day journey to the harbor was long and exhausting. By the time they stopped to camp near the sea on the second day, Airell's back ached from riding a horse and her arms felt like jelly from holding the reigns. She was used to horseback riding, but the steady march across the countryside had been relentless.

They only stopped for a midday meal that day and then the army split. Half of them headed north with Lord Caerul and although Airell feared for the northern kingdoms in their path, she was relieved to see the tall, blond soldier disappear over the hills. Something about him made her skin crawl.

She continued west with the other half of the army, led by King Malcolm. She rode next to Prince Tiernay the entire time, but barely heard a word out of him. He kept the same solemn expression as when she first saw him. However, he *did* treat her like a lady and didn't stare at her with hungry eyes like his uncle.

When they stopped for the day, he dismounted his

horse first and then reached to help her down. A slight blush spread across her cheeks as he gripped her waist. She braced her hands on his shoulders until her feet hit solid ground.

"Thank you, Milord," she murmured, but he avoided her eyes and walked away as fast as he'd appeared.

Airell frowned, watching his hasty retreat. Then she walked toward the cliffs overlooking the sea. What about her looks or personality repulsed him so much? She was unaccustomed to people ignoring her and Prince Tiernay was her betrothed. Airell couldn't imagine being married to someone who never wanted to carry on a conversation.

Her irritated thoughts were cut short when she looked over the cliffs. Airell smelled a hint of smoke on the breeze and then saw the large fleet of enemy ships. Debris and dead bodies floated in the water around them. What had once been the bustling seaside harbor of Áthas, full of fishermen and merchants selling goods, had now been reduced to ruins and death. The surrounding village had been pillaged and burned as well.

Airell turned away and covered her mouth to stifle a sob. It was no wonder there hadn't been a soul to warn them of the eminent attack on the castle. Áthas had been caught by complete surprise.

"Your tent is ready, if you would like to rest before dinner, Your Majesty," a servant boy informed her.

She wiped her eyes and thanked the ginger-haired boy who appeared no older than twelve. Then she followed him to the place she would sleep for the night.

Stepping into the tent, she was relieved to see her trunk of belongings had been brought in like the night before and a small bedroll had already been laid out with fur blankets and a pillow. It looked so inviting, she opted to retire early and skip the evening meal. After seeing the ruins of Áthas, she didn't have much of an appetite anyway.

Airell removed her outer tunic and boots, grateful her ladies had packed her some practical traveling clothes that didn't require help to untie in the back. Then she crawled under the fur blankets, pulling them all the way up to her chin. The ground was hard and rocky underneath her bedroll, but at least she had some kind of cushion underneath as a barrier. Weary from travelling and grief, Airell thought she would fall asleep as soon as her head hit the pillow, but instead, she could only stare at the top of her temporary chambers while the light faded from the sky.

A few guards were posted outside of her tent, but she didn't trust any of them yet. Also, thoughts of her family and friends back at the castle tormented her. She requested at least one of her maids accompany her if they wished, but King Malcolm refused, gruffly informing her she would have new maids in his land. Now her heart ached to talk with the dear friends she'd had from childhood. They knew her better than anyone and would understand her agonizing longing for home.

Finally, after moistening her pillow with a few lonely tears, Airell fell into a restless sleep.

The next morning, they were all up before the dawn. Airell watched as the men busied themselves disassembling tents and loading supplies onto the ships. She counted over two dozen, noticing most of them were long warships with rows, while only two had sails, built for long voyages and seemed to have living quarters.

Hearing commotion, Airell turned and noticed King Malcolm and Prince Tiernay in the middle of a heated discussion. Progress at getting the ships ready ceased while they argued.

The prince had his arms crossed over his chest in defiance. "'Tis not proper, Uncle! I would at least like to retain my sense of propriety!"

The king scoffed and stomped away in anger before summoning two guards nearby. After receiving orders, they walked toward the ruins of Áthas and returned half an hour later, but they weren't alone. They drug a man in a long gray robe with them while navigating the craggy hill by the shore. She recognized him as the priest in the village. When they came closer, she noticed a gash above his right eyebrow and tear marks on his dusty robe, evidence the guards had been unreasonably rough with the man of God.

King Malcolm's foul expression brightened at the sight and glanced at Prince Tiernay with a pleased grin. "Our traveling complication has been solved." He turned back to the priest. "My nephew, Prince Tiernay and his betrothed, Lady Airell, will be married at once."

Airell gulped down her emotions, knowing this would be coming eventually, but not quite prepared.

The guards dragged the priest to stand in front of her and then Prince Tiernay reluctantly joined them, solemn as ever.

The priest hesitated at first and then asked if she was marrying Prince Tiernay of her own free will.

A guard responded by grabbing him by the collar and the priest winced in pain. "You dare defy the king's authority?"

"Please don't hurt him!" Airell pleaded. "This is simply our custom. He is not defying the king." She turned to the frightened priest and nodded. "Aye, 'tis my choice to marry the prince in exchange for peace."

After the guard released him, the priest went on, although appearing deeply grieved, like his actions were a sin.

The ceremony was brief and the prince stared at the ground until they were asked to join hands at the end. When he did look up, his eyes were cold and his jaw clenched. It was clear he did not want any part of the arranged marriage.

However, the tension did not last long. Directly after the priest announced they were joined as husband and wife, the prince escorted her to the docks.

King Malcolm boarded the largest sailing vessel with a more regal feel, but Airell breathed a sigh of relief when Tiernay led her to the smaller and simpler sailing vessel. The thought of being away from the fierce northern king for a few days eased her mind, but there was little time to relax. Men bustled around, putting things in their correct spot and taking their positions to begin the voyage to sea. She simply stood out of the way, not sure what to do.

It did not even register with her until the ship pulled away from the docks that she was now Prince Tiernay's wife. It had all happened so quickly and not at all the wedding she imagined, but she couldn't think about her own happiness at the moment.

Airell's choice had saved her kingdom and the thought brought peace as her homeland drifted from view. Somehow she had to learn to be content in her new situation, no matter the hardships that had befallen her.

Airell shed some tears at first, but after the sorrow passed, a strange exhilarated feeling spread through her heart, not having set foot on a ship since her early childhood. Glancing at Prince Tiernay on the upper deck, she caught a hint of a fleeting smile on his face. Ever since parting ways with his uncle on the shore, she noticed his shoulders relax and the scowl ease from his handsome face. As the breeze tousled his wavy, chestnut hair, he didn't seem quite as intimidating as before. Maybe she would grow to at least tolerate this version of the prince.

The further they journeyed from shore, the exhilaration of being on a ship, morphed into something else as the waves pitched and rolled beneath her. Airell heaved over the side of the boat until she had nothing left in her stomach from breakfast. Her slight body trembled in the breeze, knees threatening to buckle beneath her.

A gentle hand rested on her upper back. "The sickness will pass after a few days, Milady."

Airell turned and weakly braced her hand against the edge of the ship. Her eyes grew wide, seeing Prince Tiernay behind her. Had he actually spoken a full sentence to her or was it a hallucination caused from her sea sickness? She gazed up into his eyes, blinking hard before determining it was really him standing before her.

Concern wrinkled his brow as he studied her pale face. "You need rest. Come, Milady. I have requested your trunk of belongings be brought into my cabin." He stopped momentarily at her horrified expression and then continued with a reassuring nod. "'Tis the only room suitable for a lady. I'll be bunking with the crew."

She agreed weakly and allowed him to guide her below deck. After stumbling down a narrow passageway, the prince opened a cabin door and motioned for her to go inside. Light filtered in from a small circular window, highlighting the simple but tidy accommodations of his cabin. A humble-sized bed sat to one side, bolted to the floorboards and covered with furs. In the shadows on the other side, she made out a small desk, cushioned chair and her trunk of belongings. "I apologize for the humble living quarters. The bed is lumpy and the window leaks a bit, but it will at least allow some privacy."

"'Tis perfectly fine," Airell murmured while sitting gingerly on the bed and clutching her churning stomach. In truth the small bed looked heavenly.

"Then I will take my leave. My servant boy will come by soon to help with whatever you need."

Lady Airell looked up as he turned to go. "Thank you, Milord."

He glanced over his shoulder for a moment, his serious expression returning as he gave a quick nod and then closed the door behind him.

Airell eased her body down on the bed, still clutching her stomach in misery, but a hint of a grin spread across her face, remembering the prince's concerned expression. Maybe there was kindness in him after all.

After a full day of traveling by sea, the exhausted prince climbed into a hammock in the crew's sleeping quarters for a few hours sleep. Tiernay didn't mind giving up his cabin for the voyage, actually finding a hammock more comfortable to sleep in while at sea. However, his eyes stared at the dark ceiling for at least an hour, thoughts wandering down the narrow passage to his old cabin. Lady Airell hadn't been seen above deck for the entire day and according to the servant, she had refused both her midday and evening meal. Before heading off to bed, Tiernay had entertained the thought of checking on her, but dismissed the notion just as quickly.

He had already given into weakness earlier in the day by helping her when a servant could have managed it. He refused to get too attached when the marriage between them would likely not last. His uncle was a cruel and manipulative man who did nothing without some sinister purpose in mind. When he looked at Lady Airell, he only pitied her. True, her bravery impressed him, but she was also naïve to believe she had the ability to create an alliance with his uncle. She'd been tricked and no documents had been signed to make the marriage alliance official.

King Malcolm had heard rumors of her beauty and had to have her. Now, she was nothing more than a prisoner of war and something else to torture Tiernay with. He'd never wanted to be involved, but had no choice now, for he was a prisoner as well—a prisoner held captive by a golden crown. Perhaps if he pretended to be indifferent to her beauty, his uncle would annul the sham of a marriage and send her back to Daireann where she belonged.

CHAPTER SEVEN

Sickness

The next couple of days at sea only became worse for Airell as a series of ruthless storms arrived. The waves rolled and pitched so violently, she feared the ship might capsize more than once. Her seasickness became even more unbearable and she couldn't hold any food or drink down. All Airell could do was clutch to the railings of her bed, heave into her chamber pot and pray God would bring her through the storm.

It went on like that for what seemed like an eternity. By the end of the third day, she had a raging headache and her stomach felt hollow and sore. Sweat beaded up on her forehead, yet even beneath the fur covers, she shivered like the temperature had dropped below freezing. She watched lightning flashing outside her window as the sea continued to roll.

When the servant boy stumbled into the room to deliver her morning meal an hour later, Airell had rolled onto the cabin floor. She was listless and bruised from her fall, barely able to lift her head.

The last thing she heard, before drifting back into a feverous state of unconsciousness, was the servant boy's gasp of surprise and the tray of food crashing to the floor.

Prince Tiernay followed the panicked servant boy below deck, stumbling and soaking wet from the rain. His heart pounded as he found the open door to his old cabin and saw the unconscious princess on the floor. The lightning revealed the outline of her pale face and while sweeping the blond hair from her face, he felt heat radiating from her sweaty forehead.

"Boy, go fetch me a wet cloth and ask the cook to fix some broth. Hurry!"

After the servant rushed off to do his bidding, Tiernay lifted Airell's limp body in his arms and carefully placed her back on the bed. His heart pounded as he paced the floor and raked his fingers through his soaked hair, furious with his uncle. Tiernay didn't know the first thing about having a lady aboard his ship. The princess was supposed to have maids to care for her—any nobleman knew that—yet the king had denied them from Lady Airell, only to be cruel. Her maids would have seen the signs and known how to help her before she became this ill.

When the servant boy returned with what he had asked for, Prince Tiernay sat on the edge of the bed, dabbing Lady Airell's forehead and neck with a cool cloth. A faint raspy breath escaped the princess's lips and her body shuddered violently, sending guilt flooding through his heart. This was *his* fault. With the storm raging outside, every man was needed on the deck to keep the ship afloat, but he should have spared a minute to check on her. The princess was his responsibility now, whether he wanted her to be or not.

"Please hold on, Milady," the prince begged while continuing to dab her forehead. "You're going to be all right."

After a few minutes, lightning flashed and Lady Airell's eyes fluttered open. She focused on his face in the dim light for a moment and then drifted off again. Tiernay recognized it as a good sign and gently brushed his fingers over her cheek, knowing she needed to drink something. "Milady, could you try some warm broth?"

She groaned and tried to lift her head, but then fell back onto her pillow again in exhaustion. The princess was too weak and her shallow breathing concerned him. Tiernay had witnessed this condition in new crew members in the past. Most recovered within a few days but one young man became so violently ill he could no longer keep down any liquids. He developed a high fever, suffered delirium and perished a few days later.

Desperate to save the princess, Tiernay threw the notion of propriety aside and gently pulled Lady Airell's pillow and upper body into his lap so she was halfway sitting up. Then, after the servant boy handed him the bowl of broth, he held a spoon of the liquid up to her lips, urging her to drink.

When she finally took a small sip, he let out a choked sigh of relief that almost sounded like a chuckle. "See, you are going to be fine." He brushed a few strands of damp hair from her forehead and his voice faltered for a moment. "I will never neglect you, nor allow any harm to come to you again. I promise."

Airell blinked several times as light filtered in

through the small window in her cabin. The ship no longer rolled and pitched, but gently swayed back and forth on the calm sea. She still felt weak and sore, but the raging headache had passed.

As her eyes drifted around the room, she vaguely remembered someone serving her warm broth and dabbing her forehead with a cool cloth during the night, waiting for her fever to break. Now, she was acutely aware that her head rested on someone's lap. Airell craned her neck and caught sight of her caretaker. He was sleeping peacefully with his head and back resting against the wall—Prince Tiernay.

Feeling her stir, his eyes opened and a relieved smile graced his lips for a moment. "Good morning, Milady. Are you feeling better?"

"Aye, a little." Airell sat up slowly with a faint groan and attempted to hide her blush.

"I'm pleased to hear it," he answered, sliding toward the edge of the bed. "Do you feel well enough to eat?"

After she said yes, he left the room and returned a few minutes later with some bread and a cup of water. She ate and drank slowly, wanting to avoid feeling ill again. When Airell finished a small piece of bread, she became aware of the prince's eyes on her as he stood across the room with his arms crossed. His concerned hazel eyes made her heart race.

She took a sip of water and gave him a nervous glance. "Did you watch over me all night?"

He nodded, looking down with a guilty expression. "Aye. You were very ill and needed special care, Milady. Your fever only abated a few hours ago. I apologize if I made you feel uncomfortable by staying."

"No, you didn't," she replied, barely above a whisper and rubbed a sore spot on her shoulder where she had hit the floor in the night. "I simply wanted to thank you. I am in your debt, Milord."

Prince Tiernay shook his head, looking grieved. "There is no need to thank me, Lady Airell. 'Tis my duty to watch over you. After all, you are…" he paused for a moment, appearing to weigh his words carefully before continuing. "…a royal guest on my ship."

Airell looked away to hide the blush on her cheeks, almost wishing he would have called her his wife, but relieved he hadn't at the same time. She stayed quiet for a moment, attempting to process his sudden change of attitude toward her since they had set sail from Daireann. He seemed gentler but conflicted—almost tormented in her presence.

"Is there anything else you need before I take my leave? The crew will require my presence after being absent all night."

She considered his question, dreading the thought of remaining in the stale air of the cabin any longer. Then she peeked up at him with a hopeful look in her eyes. "Later this afternoon, some fresh air might do me some good."

CHAPTER EIGHT

Life at Sea

Prince Tiernay lost count of how many times he had paced in front of the cabin door before it finally creaked open. When Lady Airell appeared in the doorway he stopped and studied her for a moment. She still looked pale and weak, but much better than the previous night, wearing a simple sky blue gown and tunic, tied at the waist with a belt and her hair weaved into two long, golden braids.

She offered him a shy smile. "I apologize for taking so long. I am not accustomed to preparing for the day without the help of my maids."

He nodded and looked away, embarrassed she caught him staring. The prince recovered quickly and cleared his throat. "There is no need to apologize. My uncle is the one who deprived you of your maids." Bitterness had crept into his tone, so he changed the subject quickly by offering his preferred arm. "May I escort you to the upper deck?"

"Aye." She smiled and tucked her hand into the crook of his arm.

After making their way up the narrow steps, Tiernay aimed a cautious glance at the crew, observing their reactions. A few of them gawked at the young prince escorting a lady across the deck, but most went on with their business as if it made no difference to them. After a few moments, his shoulders relaxed and he realized he quite enjoyed Lady Airell's presence. In the midst of a deck full of dirty, haggard men who had battled the storm for three days and now smelled of stale sweat and fish, she was an elegant rose who graced the deck with light and beauty wherever she trod.

He led her to the edge of the ship and she wavered for a moment, but after he steadied her, they both gazed over the side. He could barely see the outline of land in the distance, surrounded by a shroud of mist.

She let out a sigh. "'Tis beautiful out here."

He nodded, relieved she finally felt well enough to enjoy it. "Aye. The sea is the only place I feel at home these days. Everything seems less…complicated out here."

She glanced over at him with a curious gleam in her cobalt blue eyes. "You do not feel at home in your own kingdom? Will you not inherit the throne in the future?"

Tiernay shrugged, not knowing how much to tell her about his complicated relationship with his uncle and his stolen birthright. Instead, he attempted to skirt around the question. "I suppose I *do* miss home. I haven't seen my mother and sister in months."

Airell's face brightened at his words. "Oh, I look forward to meeting them! How old is your sister?"

The prince swallowed a lump in his throat, remembering how his family had wept when he left. "Fiona is almost nineteen," he replied simply, wishing he had never mentioned his family. Lady Airell's recovery had lifted his spirits temporarily, but now gloom settled into his heart once more.

The princess seemed oblivious to his change of mood and told him his sister was only slightly older than her. She gazed out over the water with a contented smile on her face, no doubt looking forward to some female companionship once they arrived. "Tell me about your land. Is it colder than Daireann?"

He nodded and continued the conversation, not wanting to ruin her pleasant mood. "Aye, quite a bit colder in the fall and winter. When we arrive, you will require a different wardrobe to last you through the snowy season." Noticing her frown and visibly shiver, he continued with something more encouraging. "However, the spring and summer are enjoyable. The cliffs over the northern sea are a magnificent sight and there are gulls and puffins nesting by them and seals sun themselves on the rocks as well."

Airell's smile returned. "It sounds lovely."

"Aye," he agreed, gazing out at the moving sea and remembering his childhood fondly—searching the beach for shells with his sister and laughing at the gulls as they scurried to find tiny fish wriggling in the surf. "It was."

Airell stared at him in confusion for a moment, obviously recognizing he spoke in past tense. However the prince didn't correct himself or explain further. He couldn't bring himself to tell her the whole truth yet.

Over the next three days, Airell grew more comfortable with sailing. She had finally managed to find her sea legs and her stomach felt less queasy. Airell also enjoyed her conversations with the prince, even though she could sense he held things back from her.

They fell into an odd sort of new routine with each other. In the morning after breakfast, he escorted her to the upper deck and they strolled while talking, mostly about her family back in Daireann. Tiernay seemed reluctant to divulge very much about his family, but they did talk about some of his favorite places to visit in his kingdom. Then in the evening before dinner, they repeated the routine. Sometimes they spent time watching the dolphins as they leapt out of the water by the prow of the ship, almost as if they were having a race. She avoided any deep conversation for the time being, but slowly they were beginning to grow more at ease in each other's company.

In the afternoons when the prince became busy with his duties, Lady Airell spent her time getting acquainted with the servant boy. He was painfully shy at first, but by their fifth day at sea she discovered he was eleven and his name was Slade. He had been left orphaned after his parents died from a sudden illness. Shortly after, Prince Tiernay took him on as one of his servants.

Sometimes after Slade served her lunch, she invited him to stay and eat with her. Then afterwards she read him adventurous tales from a leather bound book she had in her trunk of belongings. The stories were the same ones she made up and read to Gwyn in the evenings before bedtime. He loved them so much, one afternoon she offered to lend him the book.

He shook his head, appearing shy. "Thank you, Your Majesty. I would love to, but I'm afraid I cannot read."

Airell frowned. "Oh, I see. Well that simply won't

do." She looked down for a moment and bit her lip, deep in thought. When she looked up, her eyes gleamed with excitement. "I could teach you!"

The boy shifted nervously on his feet. "I'm not sure the king would allow it."

She lifted her eyebrows in defiance. "Well, thankfully the king is not aboard this ship, is he?" The boy grinned as she gave him a playful wink. "If you change your mind and wish to learn, meet me near the stairs after you finish your afternoon duties.

Prince Tiernay finished discussing their course for the next day with the captain and went off in search of Lady Airell to prepare her. His lips formed a stern line, dreading the next day. They would be arriving in Órlaith and things would change when they were in the presence of his uncle again. He wanted to warn her, however, when he knocked on her door, she didn't answer. His heart pounded while navigating the stairs and he started to panic while searching the upper deck. However, after asking around, he was finally directed to a secluded spot near the stern behind some barrels and found Airell sitting on the deck with the servant boy. She held a book in her hand while pointing out letters and having him repeat the sounds they made. When Tiernay appeared, the boy looked up with wide, terrified eyes.

On edge from worrying about Airell and the prospect of arriving in Órlaith the next day, Tiernay over reacted and lifted the boy by his shoulders a little rougher than he meant to. "Get up, boy. If you will not pull your weight around this ship, I'll throw you overboard. Now get back to work!" The servant cowered away from him and then scurried off.

Lady Airell stared at Prince Tiernay. Her eyes were wide with shock at first and then narrowed in contempt as she snapped her book shut. "Was that necessary? He's only a child! Besides, it was my idea to teach him to read. Be angry at me if you must, but don't take it out on an innocent child."

Tiernay closed his eyes for a moment, trying to rein in his temper, but when he opened them again, his tone still bristled with irritation. "Aye, he *is* a child, but more importantly a *servant.* Teaching the boy to read will only harm him in the end."

"His name is *Slade.*" Lady Airell's eyes flamed at him as she stood and dusted off her gown. "My father always said being well-educated was a benefit to all people, even the lowliest servants in our kingdom."

The prince sighed and his voice softened but still resonated with authority. "I apologize for being blunt, Milady, but we are no longer *in* your kingdom. Unfortunately, you will have to learn to adjust to our way of life, whether you agree with it or not. Your safety depends on it."

The princess scoffed and shouldered past him in disgust.

Tiernay watched her disappear below deck and then hung his head in despair, wishing he would have handled the situation with more discretion. Why did he long to please her so much? A foreboding ache knotted his stomach. Would his weakness in Lady Airell's presence turn out to be his fatal flaw?

CHAPTER NINE

Restless

Lady Reagan entered the royal chambers with a sealed letter in hand. She expected to see her husband resting, but instead she found him pacing before the window, still wearing the sling the physician had given him. Seeing him wince now, she feared he had aggravated the healing wound in his side.

She crossed the room and gripped his arm. "Arlan, the physician said you require rest."

He turned to her and managed a weak smile. "Aye, but he also recommended I take walks."

She nodded and cupped his pale cheek in her hand. "Relaxing walks, my love...not restless ones."

His tired eyes gazed into hers. "I apologize, Reagan. I simply cannot relax while knowing my sister is sailing north with those monsters." He looked down at her free hand, noticing the letter. "What is this?"

She sighed, fearing the contents of the letter would only bring him additional anxiety. "'Tis from Áthas."

His eyes widened in anticipation. "Does it contain

word of my sister's well-being?"

Tears stung Reagan's eyes. "Aye, I believe so." She broke the wax seal and handed it to him.

"Arlan's blue eyes scanned the letter and then he clenched the paper in his fist. "'Tis signed by a priest in the village. He was forced to officiate the wedding between my sister and Prince Tiernay. He said she did nothing to protest the marriage, but they were in such a hurry to set sail, no papers were signed to make the marriage alliance official."

"What does that mean?"

"She was tricked into marrying the prince in exchange for peace. The priest says it seemed as though he was forced to marry her. It could be grounds for an annulment. Somehow we must find a way to rescue her!"

Reagan's breath caught in her throat. "My husband, our army is worn thin. So many deaths—so many injuries. They need time to recover and so do you."

"I know this, but I cannot abandon my sister. She is nothing but a prisoner of war—a trophy. What hardships will she encounter—what unimaginable horrors?" He covered his contorting face with his palm for a moment and then began to cough.

She pulled on his elbow gently. "We will think of something, but first you must concentrate on your health. You are not helping Airell by neglecting yourself. She needs you to be strong."

"Aye, you're right," he finally agreed before sputtering out another cough and allowing her to lead him back to the bed.

After he was settled, she tucked the covers around him and placed his favorite book within reach on the nightstand. "Try to rest. While I'm gone, I'll ask the physician for an herbal remedy to sooth your cough."

He gazed at her with gratitude in his tired, cobalt eyes. "What would I do without you, my dear wife? Will you not stay and rest with me for a while? You look weary as well."

She leaned down and kissed his forehead, pausing to caress his cheek before rising to her full height again. "I will return in an hour. Your mother and sister will visit soon if you should need anything."

After he nodded and closed his eyes, Reagan left the room and leaned against the door with her eyes closed. So much responsibility had been placed on her shoulders, she felt her knees would buckle under the weight. First the siege and acting as regent for her husband. On top of that, nursing a reluctant patient had taken its toll on her.

"Reagan?" She opened her eyes and saw Arlan's youngest sister, Gwyneth staring up at her. The young women's hazel doe eyes filled with concern. "Has my brother's condition worsened?"

She shook her head, attempting a reassuring smile to comfort the girl. She had to be lonely since Airell had left with the enemy's company. They had always been inseparable. "He has only developed a mild cough," she reassured. "The physician will return soon with some medicine."

Gwyneth's shoulders relaxed. "Oh, I'm glad to hear it. May I sit with him?"

"Of course, Gwyn. I'm sure he would enjoy talking with you." She patted the girl's shoulder. "But first, how is your mother?"

She sighed and fidgeted with the long raven braid hanging over one of her shoulders. "She is not well. After my father died, she was the strong one for all of

us, but this has broken her. She clings to my sister's letter at night and weeps until falling asleep. I think she
blames herself for not making Airell stay in the secret
passage with us during the siege."

Reagan bit her lip, fighting tears. "I blame myself
for that as well. I allowed her to go with me to the infirmary."

Gwyn drew in a ragged breath and took both
Reagan's hands in hers. "See, that is where both of you
are mistaken. No one is to blame, except King Malcolm. He is the enemy and we must work together to
defeat him, instead of placing blame on ourselves."

Reagan nodded and wiped her tears, amazed at how
much Gwyn had matured in only a few short days. She
spoke with wisdom equal to someone twice her age.
"Aye, you are right." She hugged the girl close before
holding her at arm's length and offering a proud smile.
"You will make a fine queen one day, Lady Gwyneth."

Her eyes brightened. "Do you really think so?"

"Aye, of that I am certain."

Once Gwyneth went into the royal chambers,
Reagan headed down the hallway to her study. Behind
closed doors, she took a seat behind her desk and
penned a letter in secret code, asking her cousin, the
regent of South Rhona to send some of the Daireann
soldiers back home. It was a daring move to ask Lord
Fergus to send them, knowing their country would
need all the soldiers they could get if King Malcolm decided to attack, however she deemed it a necessary risk,
for the good of the people of Daireann. With their king
ill and young men injured or dead, spirits were low.
They needed some hope. They needed their brave princess to be returned home safely and Reagan was determined to make it happen.

CHAPTER TEN

Ruins

Prince Tiernay woke up the next morning blurry-eyed and tense. In truth, he had barely slept as guilt tormented him over the way he had spoken with Lady Airell the previous day. He wanted to avoid her altogether, but knew he still needed to prepare her for their arrival in Órlaith. So, like clockwork after breakfast, he knocked on her door and then waited outside it like usual for their morning stroll on the deck.

When she came out a few moments later, she didn't look angry as he feared, but offered him a shy smile instead. "Good morning, Milord. I trust you slept well?"

He rubbed his eyes and looked away. It almost would have been easier if she *were* angry at him. Now he felt like a monster and needed to make amends. Clutching his hands behind his back, he finally looked into her innocent cobalt eyes. "Before we take our stroll, I need to ask for your forgiveness, Lady Airell. I overreacted and understand if you are still upset with me."

She gave him a knowing look and her smile returned. "I have already forgiven you, Prince Tiernay."

He blinked hard. "You have?"

She nodded. "Does not the Scripture say, 'Let not the sun go down upon your wrath?'"

"Aye, Milady. I believe it does," he replied, staring at her in amazement. He remembered the verse from Ephesians 4:26 well because of his many tutors as a child, but recalled very few who could actually put the concept into practice. The prince recovered quickly and offered his preferred arm. "Shall we?"

She agreed and soon they had made their way up to the deck in silence as Tiernay thought over their conversation. He had never met anyone who fascinated him like Princess Airell. When they reached the side of the deck, he gulped down his pride and turned to her. "I have been thinking about what you said yesterday about the boy…" he stopped for a moment at her raised eyebrow before correcting himself. "I mean about *Slade*…and have decided it will be acceptable for you to teach him to read."

"Really?" She beamed in his direction and gave him an impulsive kiss on the cheek, making them both blush in surprise.

He glanced sideways to see if anyone took notice and then looked back at her. "Aye, but you must be discreet. The king must not hear word of this."

She tried to keep a straight face and nodded, clutching her hands together in an attempt to look proper. "Of course, Milord."

"And the lessons mustn't resume until we return to the ship tomorrow," he added. "There will be too many prying eyes once we go ashore."

She nodded and then studied his face with a furrowed brow. "Return to the ship?"

"I apologize, I meant to tell you yesterday, we will be staying the night in Órlaith. King Malcolm wishes to collect more gold from the ruins."

The mood turned somber and Tiernay wished he could take back his words. He knew her father had died in Órlaith and it would be an emotional time for her. However, she needed to know the truth, regardless of her feelings.

She turned pale and swallowed hard. "Will we stay in the castle?"

He looked at her with a grave expression. "I do not know what the king has planned, but you may remain on the ship if you wish. A few servants and guards will also remain onboard."

She gazed out over the gentle waves with a far off look in her eyes, watching the land grow bigger on the horizon. When she glanced back at him, her eyes looked misty and sad, but determined. "No, I wish to stay with you."

Arriving in Órlaith proved to be nothing less than devastating for Airell. What had once been known as the Golden Kingdom, had now been abandoned—the walls crumbling and the surrounding village reduced to ash. The castle was still intact for the most part, but occupied by members of the king's army.

When she saw King Malcolm stepped off his ship with a pompous grin on his face, she couldn't help seething beneath the surface. *He* had done this to the innocent people of Órlaith. He had caused her father's death. He had murdered, Tristan and his family—and for what? Power and riches. She struggled to hide her hatred toward the evil king, knowing her thoughts weren't very Christian in nature.

By the time Prince Tiernay escorted her off his ship, Airell had managed to compose herself, keeping her raw emotions hidden behind a forced smile. When they approached the king, she curtsied and kissed his ring, like a proper lady.

King Malcolm's proud smile sickened her. "Welcome to the great Kingdom of Órlaith, Milady. It does not appear grand at the moment, but we will rebuild. Perhaps after a few years, I will give it to you both as a belated wedding gift."

She glanced at the prince whose gaze pleaded for her silence.

"You are most generous, Uncle," Tiernay replied with a slight bow.

The king studied him with curious eyes and then looked back at her. "Well, I'm pleased to see my nephew is in a better mood, thanks to you, Princess."

She froze again, not sure how to reply, but thankfully, the king turned with a swish of his crimson robe and walked toward the castle entrance, wordlessly expecting them to follow. Tiernay offered his arm and she took it with a trembling hand.

"You're doing well," he whispered while they walked. "Just stay close to me and everything will be fine."

She held his arm tighter, amazed at how quickly she had come to trust him. It was probably foolish, since she had only known him for a sennight, but at the moment she felt safe by his side.

Stepping inside the courtyard, Airell smelled the rotting dead bodies before she saw them. Her stomach churned and she swallowed a lump in her throat, unsure if she could go forward.

Sensing her apprehension, Prince Tiernay wrapped his arm around her shoulders, pulling her head close to his chest to shield her from the sight. "Don't look." She closed her eyes and allowed him to lead her blindly through the courtyard. "Almost there," he whispered a few moments later. Then, after what seemed like an eternity he released her. "'Tis safe to look now."

She opened her eyes and saw they stood in front of the castle entrance with about half a dozen soldiers standing nearby.

"Who's in charge here?" King Malcolm shouted, face red with anger.

A tall, muscular soldier stepped forward and bowed before him. "Doughlas, at your service, Your Majesty."

"Ah yes...*Doughlas,* how long did you have to prepare for our arrival?" The king's voice was low, but intimidating.

The guard's eyes shifted back and forth nervously. "A fortnight, Milord."

"Aye, *a fortnight.* So, you had an ample amount of time to prepare the castle for our arrival, yet there are still bodies in the courtyard?" There is a lady present— my nephew's new bride. Were you aware of that?"

"N....no. I didn't know, Your Majesty. I apologize. There were so many bodies, it took longer than expected."

The king started to pace in front of the man, hands clutched behind his back. He wore a smile on his face but his dark eyes were cold and hard. "What do you think makes a good leader, Doughlas?"

"I...I don't know, Milord."

"Someone who takes their responsibilities seriously. Someone who doesn't make petty excuses. So, after my little lecture, do you believe you are a good leader?"

The soldier hung his head and his hands began to shake. "N-no, Milord, b-but I can do better. Please forgive me."

King Malcolm sneered, looking like a fierce wild boar. "One failure is too many." In one quick motion, the king drew his sword.

Airell let out a muffled scream of horror as Tiernay pulled her against his chest again to shield her from the sight, but it didn't mask the awful squelching noise and a groan of pain as the king plunged his sword into the soldier. She had never witnessed a king showing such brutality toward his own people.

"Now you have another body to dispose of!" the king shouted at the other men. "Get this all cleaned up before nightfall or you will join him!"

Airell shook like a leaf and clung to the prince as he led her past the dead man and into the castle. Scattered leaves and dust blew across the stone floor and she noticed a few faint blood stains, but thankfully no more bodies.

However, they hadn't walked two feet before hearing commotion from around the corner. Soon one of the king's guards appeared with a young girl struggling to get free from his vice grip.

"What is the meaning of this?" the king demanded.

"I found this one hiding in the kitchen, Your Majesty. She's a thief." The girl started to whimper as the guard put her down but gripped her hair this time to keep her from moving. "What would you have me do with her?"

Airell's heart lurched. The girl looked to be about ten and deathly thin, like she hadn't eaten a proper meal in months.

"We have no need for thieves here, not with so much treasure at stake in these ruins" King Malcolm flicked his hand to the side dismissively. "Take her outside and dispose of her quietly."

The girl squealed in terror as the guard started to drag her outside. "I'm not a thief. I'm a maid and I was only hungry. I can do whatever you wish...cook, clean, wash clothes...anything you need! Please, don't kill me."

"I'm in need of a maid!" Airell blurted out.

Both the king and prince turned to her in surprise.

She nodded and explained, stuttering at first. "I-I do. It...it has been difficult to get along without someone helping me in the mornings and evenings. You see, most of my dresses tie up the back where I can't reach. I'm afraid I've been quite a burden to Prince Tiernay with how long I take to get ready." Airell stopped abruptly, realizing she had been babbling, but couldn't bear the thought of any more bloodshed.

The king stroked his beard, appearing to think it over, before Prince Tiernay spoke up. "'Tis true, Uncle. She has been quite a burden, indeed." He paused before briefly glancing at Airell, his eyes silently telling her he didn't mean it, before continuing. "It would be much easier if she had a maid."

Finally the king nodded. "Very well, but the first time this *maid* causes mischief, it will be over, understand?"

The guard released the girl and she curtsied. "Thank you, Your Majesty. I won't cause any trouble. I promise."

"Good." He paused and rubbed his temples, wincing in anguish and then flung his arm to one side. "Now, out of my sight before I change my mind. Go prepare my nephew and his wife appropriate chambers for the night."

As the girl dashed up the stairs to do his bidding, Airell aimed an exhausted grin in Tiernay's direction. After the day's events, she knew they weren't just dealing with a ruthless king. He had fallen into complete madness. However, even though her body still trembled because of the whole ordeal, she couldn't help feeling victorious in her heart. At least with the help of the prince, she had convinced King Malcolm to show mercy toward the girl. It was a good start.

CHAPTER ELEVEN

Monsters

Within an hour, Slade and Airell's new maid, Isla, had worked together to prepare chambers for her. It was a grand room with tall golden archways and a large four poster bed with an intricately woven lavender bedspread. Two guards carried in her trunk of belongings and Slade started lugging in warm buckets of water to fill a tub so she could have a proper bath.

When the bath was ready, Airell slipped into it, relishing how good it felt to scrub all the dirt and grime off her after a week traveling at sea. However, after a moment, her eyes darted around the room in dismay, seeing dolls, horse figurines and hair ribbons scattered among shelves. The chambers had probably belonged to a young girl—a member of the royal family who was deceased. She had most likely suffered a violent death at the hands of King Malcolm's army.

She quickly washed her hair, dried off and dressed in her white shift. Then Airell wasted no time calling Isla in to help her prepare for dinner. She didn't want to remain in the room alone any longer than necessary.

The girl walked in with a timid smile, looking much better than before. She had her dark hair pulled into two long braids and found some clean clothes from one of the other chambers to put on. Isla brushed Airell's hair and then helped her into a rose gown she had laid out on the bed.

"My mother used to have lovely gowns like this…I mean she had a pink dress with a similar shade," the girl corrected while helping tighten the laces on the back. "Her gowns weren't nearly as fancy of course, but I enjoyed helping her dress up when our kingdom had special occasions."

"That's nice, Isla. I'm sure she loves you very much. Where is she now? Were you separated?"

Isla sniffled behind her. "My mother died after the attack on Órlaith. She became ill and I couldn't find medicine or enough food."

Airell turned around and hugged Isla, heart breaking with the young girl. "I'm so sorry. I can't imagine what you must have gone through, but you're under my care now. I promise to watch over you like an elder sister would."

The girl thanked her and continued to weep for several minutes before composing herself and beginning to arrange Airell's hair for the evening. In the end, when Isla had finished, she looked in the mirror and felt pleased with the intricate cage braid trailing down to her waist. Not only that, it was wonderful to have some female companionship again.

When a knock from the adjoining room interrupted them, Airell answered it. The prince stared at her for a long time and then smiled. "You look lovely tonight, Milady."

She grinned. "Oh, you're just unaccustomed to seeing me in anything other than traveling clothes."

She took a moment to study him as well. He looked rather dashing in a fresh tunic and cloak.

However, Isla's reaction puzzled her. The poor girl's hands trembled and her eyes filled with terror. Sure, Airell had been intimidated by the prince at their first meeting as well, but he had helped save Isla's life downstairs only a few hours ago.

"Isla, are you feeling unwell?"

"I'm fine, Your Majesty," she said and then darted off to the far corner of the room, pretending to tidy something up.

Airell, dismissed her maid's odd behavior and bid her farewell before the prince escorted her down the hallway. Maybe Isla was just tired and still grieving over her mother. She'd mention it later and find out what was bothering the young girl.

"How are you, tonight?" Tiernay asked while they descended the stairs.

"I'm a little better, but I still can't stop thinking of all the people who perished here," she whispered in the echoing halls. "This place feels like a tomb."

He hung his head for a moment at the hollow tone of her voice. "I know. I didn't want to stay here either, but at least we will have a decent meal tonight. I heard the king has arranged for quite a feast. I do hope you will try to eat something. We have another sennight of travel and you will need to keep your strength up."

A faint smile bloomed on Airell's lips. Even though they were under a tremendous amount of stress, not to mention, trapped in a tomb of a castle for the evening, the prince still worried about her well-being.

Tiernay studied her with curious eyes. "What is it?"

The princess turned to him in admiration before they descended the stairs together. "The past few days have proven first impressions can be wrong. 'Tis a pleasant surprise, I suppose."

His brow furrowed. "I'm afraid I don't understand."

Her smile grew bigger at his humble confusion. "*You*, Milord," she whispered. "*You* have pleasantly surprised me."

After escorting Lady Airell back to her room for the night, Prince Tiernay journeyed back into his room with a smile on his face. The dinner had been unexpectedly carefree, mostly due to the fact his uncle had indulged in too much wine before they arrived. He was full of humor and cheer, unlike his usual gruff and cruel countenance and then retired early, leaving Tiernay to dine with Lady Airell alone.

She had been a pleasant companion to enjoy the evening with, even though they were both uneasy about staying in the ruins. During the hour they spent together, all their anxiety seemed to fade away and for the first time, Tiernay caught a glimpse of what a future would be like with Lady Airell as his wife.

Now, as he journeyed to the terrace outside his temporary chambers overlooking the ruins of the once great kingdom, his smile faded and darkness consumed him. Tiernay knew it was a foolish notion to believe he could have a happy future. It was only a matter of time before Lady Airell discovered his involvement in the fall of Órlaith.

His mind drifted back to the day he left with his uncle for war—how his mother had clung to him, begging King Malcolm not to take him, but his uncle had refused with a cruel and cold look in his dark eyes.

His mother's last words to Tiernay before setting sail tormented him every day. "Don't give in, my son. Don't let him change you, no matter what." She had tears in her eyes as she placed a trembling hand over the left side of his chest. "You have a good heart beating within you—so pure and full of love. Remember that."

His chin quivered in the darkness, knowing he had failed her. The battle of Órlaith *had* changed him. Tiernay closed his eyes, trying to block out the memories of fiery arrows, clashing swords and gurgled screams of the night King Malcolm's army attacked the kingdom. It was futile. His guilt would never lessen because he had done nothing to stop their destruction.

During the battle, his uncle forced him to do something even more sinister—something that would haunt him for the rest of his days. If he had refused, King Malcom would have murdered his mother and sister out of spite. His uncle had warped Tiernay's pure love for his family into a dark and morbid motivation to kill an innocent.

He still had nightmares about the battle, but his uncle had given him no choice. That was how he justified it, but now he knew the bitter truth. He had turned into a monster, like Malcolm.

He remembered what Airell had told him early in the night—that he had pleasantly surprised her. He recalled the innocence and admiration in her eyes and now it stung into him like a thousand arrows. She believed him to be a good man and her belief shined a beam of light back into his darkened heart. For the short time they had known each other, Tiernay thought perhaps his soul was redeemable. Now he knew better. Whatever the princess thought she saw in him was a lie. Once she found out who he really was and the awful things he'd done, she would never grow to love him. Who could ever learn to love a monster?

CHAPTER TWELVE

No Escape

The next morning and afternoon went by quickly for Airell as the men loaded gold and other treasures onto the boats and prepared for their departure. She stayed in her temporary chambers for most of the morning. Prince Tiernay had made himself scarce after breakfast while helping to supervise. When he finally returned, Airell breathed a sigh of relief. However, she couldn't help noticing something different about him. He still offered his arm to escort her to his ship, yet his face seemed gloomy and tormented again.

"Is everything all right?" she whispered.

He forced a smile and patted her hand. "I am only anxious to sail away from this place."

She accepted his answer, knowing she would feel much better once safely aboard his ship as well. However, even after they set off, Tiernay's serious expression remained. He seemed on edge and gruff with his crew members, which was unlike him.

That night, Airell decided her new maid, Isla, would

sleep in her cabin. It was the only suitable option and although it was cramped on her bed, she didn't want the girl sleeping on the floor. It was nice at first, as Isla reminded her of her sister Gwyn and they kept each other warmer. However as the night wore on, Airell became aware of Isla's trembling and whimpers in her sleep.

"Isla," she whispered gently. "Isla wake up."

The girl opened her eyes and Airell noticed tears glistening on her cheeks in the moonlight.

"What troubles you?"

The girl sniffled and turned away with her back toward her. "'Tis nothing, Your Majesty."

Airell frowned. "No, please tell me."

Isla sighed and her body began to tremble. "I'm afraid."

She ran her fingers through the girl's hair—the same way she used to calm her younger sister. "You needn't be afraid. The mad king is far away for now, on another ship...and when we arrive in his kingdom I will protect you."

Isla shook her head. "'Tis not the king who causes me to tremble tonight, but the prince."

"The prince?" Airell released a light chuckle. "There is no reason to be scared of him. He is different than King Malcolm—kind and gentle." A smile spread across her face involuntarily, thinking about the way he looked at her during dinner the previous evening.

"He is a merciless killer too...same as the king."

Airell shook her head in disbelief. "You must be mistaken. Do not believe everything you hear, Isla. He is a good man."

Isla turned toward her in the moonlight, her face pinched with grief. "I saw it with my own two eyes,

Your Majesty. During the attack on Órlaith, he confronted my cousin, the prince."

She let out an alarmed gasp. "Prince Tristan was your cousin?"

"Aye," the girl bit her trembling bottom lip before continuing. "I apologize for lying yesterday. What I told you about my mother dying after the fall of Órlaith is true, but I didn't tell you King Donovan was my uncle. The Dark Lord beheaded him on the battlefield." The girl started to sob and Airell held her close.

"'Tis all right. You don't have to tell me everything if it's too painful and I won't tell anyone you are a part of the royal family."

"Thank you," the girl whispered and then leaned back, wiping her eyes. "But you need to know, Prince Tiernay is not who he seems. He pursued Prince Tristan up the cliff and tried to kill him." Airell could only stare in disbelief, not believing him to be capable of such a thing. "After the prince's blade sliced across his chest, my cousin stumbled back and fell into the sea."

Airell's eyes filled with tears, imagining the pain and fear he must have experienced before dying. "Prince Tristan was to be my betrothed. If he hadn't perished that day, we would have been family, Isla. I'm so sorry you had to watch it happen." She buried her face in the pillow as bitter tears of grief and betrayal overtook her. Could it really be true? Had she married the same man who murdered her betrothed?

Isla gripped her arm. "Lady Airell, my cousin lives."

She sat up and wiped her eyes, heartbeat quickening. "He survived the fall? How?"

"By some miracle, I suppose. I fled the castle with my mother, but after she fell ill and passed away, I returned. In my old room I found a coded message from my brother, Leland, saying he and Tristan had survived. He urged me to journey back to Kiely in the mountains and take refuge there with the other surviving members of our kingdom."

Relief filled her and then a startling realization. "So, Tristan is now the King of Órlaith." Airell slid off the bed, lit the candle on the desk and began packing a few essentials from her trunk into a leather satchel. Her heart ached with hurt and grief. Prince Tiernay had been deceiving her the entire time. If he kept this secret from her, what else did he hide? Was their marriage treaty even valid?

Isla watched her with wide eyes. "Your Majesty, what are you doing?"

Airell spoke in a quiet raspy tone, hardly able to breathe. "Gather your things. We need to escape and find King Tristan in the mountains. He is our only hope. Do you know the way to Kiely?"

The girl nodded, trembling in the moonlight. "Aye, 'twas my mother's village, but how will we navigate to the shore?"

Airell's heartbeat thumped loud in her ears, fearing her own plan and remembering she didn't want to leave without Slade. She had grown to think of the servant as a younger brother and somehow she had to save him, too. She looked in Isla's direction, faking confidence. "I'll worry about that part."

Tiernay wasn't sure what awakened him, but he had rolled out of his hammock and landed with his feet on the floor in a fragment of a second, hand on the pummel of his sword.

Then he heard it—a faint scraping noise from the

deck above. He slipped on his boots, crept out of the room and navigated up the narrow stairs in the darkness. Then with the moonlight as a guide, he headed toward the stern of the ship, where he guessed the sound had originated from. A few guards patrolled the upper deck, but he avoided them, hoping to keep the advantage of surprise over the intruder.

At first he didn't see anything, but then a tiny shimmer of gold behind a barrel caught his eye. He rushed over to where he saw it and came face to face with Airell, holding a dagger inches from his chest.

"Don't come any closer," she warned, eyes wide and intense in the moonlight.

He dropped his sword and put his hands up in a nonthreatening manner, puzzled by her sudden fear of him. "I'm not going to hurt you, Milady. I only wish to prevent you from making a reckless decision. Please, put the blade down."

Her hand trembled as she spoke. "S-step back, Milord. You can stop pretending now. I know who you really are…and what you did to my betrothed, Prince Tristan."

He glanced to the side for the first time, noticing Slade and Isla waited in a rowboat suspended above the water. Then it finally hit him—the way Isla had been looking at him the other evening. She remembered him. Somehow she saw him kill the prince and now Airell knew as well, but he couldn't let her go. "You must be fearful of me now and have every reason to be," he reasoned in a soft voice. "But I only desire to protect you. Please believe me when I say you will not survive out there on your own. Winter is coming soon and journeying through the mountains will be treacherous."

She lowered her blade for a moment, appearing to

think over his words, but then the running footsteps of guards filled his ears, drawn by the commotion.

Tiernay turned to look at the guards armed with swords and then back at Lady Airell who had jumped onto a platform to board the row boat. He leapt after the princess to shield her.

Surprised by his sudden movement, she jabbed the dagger into his shoulder in defense.

He cried out at the sudden fiery pain and held onto her waist in a vain attempt to steady his balance. But it was too late and his momentum sent them both plummeting backwards off the edge of the ship.

Air rushed from below as they fell, still clutched together in an awkward embrace. Then icy needles seemed to pierce through his entire body as they slammed into the water full force. For a moment he could only think of the pain and they both sunk under the waves like a dead weight. Then, after a moment when he came to his senses, Tiernay kicked off his boots and clutched onto Airell's arm, pulling her toward the surface with him.

When his head surged above the water and he gasped for breath, his first thought was of Lady Airell. He sputtered and shivered, gagging on bitter salt water while trying to keep her head above water as they bobbed up and down in the waves. "Milady!" When she didn't respond, his heart sunk. "Lady Airell…open your eyes!" Tiernay's eyes stung as his own tears mixed with the ocean water on his face.

When the ship finally turned, one of his guards, Peadar, dove into the sea. Then he helped Tiernay lift Airell's lifeless body out of the water and into the hands of the crew members hanging from a rope ladder.

After crawling up to safety himself a few moments

later, a sob of despair escaped his throat, observing her limp form resting on the wooden deck. She was unresponsive and turning blue, surrounded by his sorrowful crew.

Tiernay crawled toward the princess and lifted her upper body into his lap. He held Lady Airell sideways and patted her back hard. Somehow he had to expel the water from her lungs.

"God, please help me!"

The prayer came out of nowhere, surprising him. Tiernay hadn't talked to God since his father's death.

After a few long and tense moments, her body lurched forward and sea water gurgled out of her mouth before she coughed and sucked in a few ragged breaths.

"Thank you, God! Thank you!" he cried out, continuing to pat her back until her coughing subsided. She turned to look at him and at first her eyes narrowed in anger before softening. "You...you saved...me?"

He composed himself and glanced to one side, noticing over a dozen crew members gathered around them, arguing amongst themselves in confusion. He didn't know what they had seen, but he had to think of a quick cover story lest word of Airell's attempted escape reached King Malcolm's ears. "Aye, Milady. I saw you slip overboard while stargazing and I leapt in after you. I could not let my wife drown." His eyes bored into hers, silently urging her to reaffirm his story.

Her brows furrowed for a moment before a knowing expression finally came. "Aye...'twas quite foolish of me to be standing outside so late at night. Thank you for rescuing me, Milord."

Tiernay glanced upward and noticed the crew members had calmed down, satisfied with his story for the time being. The captain approached and handed them both blankets while muttering something about the folly of having females aboard the ship.

Airell sat up and looked at him, her relieved expression turning into one of alarm. "Oh, you're bleeding!" She turned to face him, inspecting the wound she had inflicted. "This is all my fault!"

"No, Milady. You are not to blame. I merely scraped my shoulder on the way down to the water," he lied, loud enough so the crew members would hear it. "'Tis...'tis only a scratch," he assured while glancing down at his throbbing shoulder. Why had it become so hard to catch his breath?

Upon closer inspection he realized the wound was deeper than he originally thought. Blood had seeped through his wet sleeve and spread all the way down his arm, dripping into a crimson pool on the deck. Dizziness plagued Tiernay and he slumped onto his side with a weak groan. Dark spots rolled around in his vision. Then, before drifting out of consciousness, he gazed upward and saw Lady Airell's beautiful face above him, crimped with worry and surrounded by a halo of stars.

CHAPTER THIRTEEN

Survivors

King Tristan grimaced and closed his eyes, leaning his back against the trunk of a large tree to catch his breath. In his mind he saw flaming arrows, smoke and death—his beloved kingdom reduced to ashes. He saw the wounded King of Daireann dying in his arms with arrows protruding from his chest. With his last breath, he pleaded with him to find his daughter and keep her safe.

Princess Airell—the breeze on the mountain seemed to whisper the beautiful name of his betrothed, yet the sound made his heart sick. Did she still live?

Tristan opened his eyes and leaned forward again, clutching his chest with a grimace. The wound was almost healed after overcoming a severe illness and fever. Now, regaining his former strength was a slow process and the wound still sent sharp pains radiating through him at times.

After a few moments, it passed and the king plucked his sword off the grass. Then he began scraping the long blade over a whetstone until it was sharpened to perfection. Tristan raised the sword and gazed at the sunlight gleaming off the smooth metal surface.

This is the blade that will avenge my father and my people. I will slay King Malcolm and Prince Tiernay if it is the last thing I do.

He gritted his teeth, remembering the Dark Prince of Brannagh—his eyes cold and unfeeling as Tristan fell wounded off the cliff and into the foaming waters below. He didn't understand why God had allowed him to survive the fall, but he liked to think He would use him to destroy the darkness hiding in the north—the darkness that had destroyed his homeland and murdered his father.

King Tristan struggled to his feet and then steadied himself against the trunk of the tree for a moment, breathing hard before heading back through the village. When the mountain fortress of Kiely came into view, his elder cousin approached, with his wolfhound trotting close behind. Leland bowed before speaking and then looked up at him with concern. "Your Majesty, I do wish you would take a few guards with you when venturing away from the fortress."

His irritation grew, but the king reined it in, remembering Leland had saved him from the water in Órlaith and tended to his wounds. "I am fine, Cousin. I simply wished to be alone. Have the men finished preparing for our departure?"

Leland's expression turned grave. "Aye, but I must plead with you again to reconsider. I can feel a change. Winter will arrive early this year."

His eyebrows lifted as he reached over and patted the wiry fur on Artair's head. The massive gray and black hound sat down and panted contently in response. "So now you are listing weather prediction among your many talents?"

His cousin shrugged with an amused grin. "The knee I injured in my youth has been aching since last week. 'Tis a sign." He moved forward and placed his hand on Tristan's shoulder, turning serious. "You need more time to recover. I say this as a brother would. I know your wound bothers you and I have witnessed your discomfort when you think no one is watching. It would be wise to wait until spring."

Tristan let out a deep sigh, considering the truth of his cousin's words. He had an ache in his bones to gather an army. He would start in Daireann and then travel to the other kingdoms and villages. Surely there were still able-bodied men in Ardena willing to fight with him. While in Daireann, he could also see Lady Airell and ask for her hand in marriage officially. He knew her brother, King Arlan, would approve of the match. An alliance with Daireann was exactly what his weakened kingdom needed right now.

As Tristan continued to think of his options, a snowflake fluttered from the sky and landed on the back of his hand. He stopped petting Artair and gazed at the flake's delicate beauty for a few moments. How could such a pure sight add so much danger to their journey? He sighed in defeat and looked over at Leland with a nod. You're right, Cousin. Traveling to Brannagh in the spring is best, but I still wish to take a small company of men to Daireann. I must know Lady Airell is safe and request the king to prepare his forces to join us. We will take refuge there for the winter if they will have us and then leave to gather a larger army in the spring."

Leland gripped his shoulder, appearing relieved at

the compromise. "Aye, Cousin and I will join you."

Lady Airell sat by Prince Tiernay's bed watching his chest rise and fall in a steady rhythm. She had stood guard over him for the rest of the night and through the morning, refusing to let any of the crew members with dirty hands get near him. Using what she had learned from her sister-in-law about caring for injuries, she cleaned the wound in his shoulder, using some of the captain's alcohol. Then she stitched it up herself with a sewing needle in her clothing trunk.

After checking his bandages, she reached for his hand and then drew back, remembering what Isla had told her about the prince and his true nature. Yet, when she looked at him, Airell also remembered his kindness toward her—how he cared for her when she had the fever—protected her in Órlaith—and saved her from drowning in the sea. She had never been so conflicted about her feelings toward someone. There had to be some good in him, but could she overlook all the bad?

"How is the prince, Your Majesty?" a deep voice asked.

She turned and saw a tall bulky guard in the doorway. The man she learned was named Peadar had to hunch over to avoid scraping his head on the doorframe. "He still hasn't awakened, but no fever has developed and his breathing seems normal."

"'Tis a good sign. I can watch over him now. You should get some rest. You went through quite an ordeal last night as well."

"I'm fine," she replied, a little more sharp than intended and paused to soften her voice. It was a good time to see where the guard's true loyalties lied. "Have you served Prince Tiernay for a long time?"

He nodded. "Aye, since he was a child. And before that, I served his father."

She sat thoughtfully for a while before speaking again. "And now you serve me."

He bowed. "Aye, 'tis an honor, Your Majesty."

"Do you have a family, Peadar?"

The guard's face dropped. "I did once, but a sickness took them from this earth."

"I'm sorry. It must be painful for you to talk about."

"'Tis all right. I have peace knowing I will see them again...and in truth, having you with us brings me comfort."

"Why?"

He gave her a sad smile. "You remind me of my daughter. She had the same faith and courage I sense in you."

Airell let out a deep sigh and smiled at the guard, realizing her first assumption of him had been wrong. "'Tis a great comfort to have another Christian aboard the ship."

"There are more, Princess Airell. You only have to look harder to find them since King Malcolm has banned Christianity in Brannagh. Give the prince a chance as well. When he thought you had drowned, I heard him praying to God for help. I believe anyone can find redemption. Don't you?"

Airell nodded, deep in thought and soon after, the guard resumed his post outside the cabin door.

When Tiernay finally opened his eyes a half an hour later, Airell decided there was only one Christian thing to do—treat him with kindness in spite of what he had done in the past. Maybe Peadar was right and she should give him another chance. She moved closer to him and talked softly, careful not to startle him. "How are you feeling?"

He stared at the ceiling and blinked several times before meeting her gaze. "Thirsty," he rasped.

Airell helped him lift his head and take a sip of water. After he rested back against his pillows again, she peeked at him in a shy manner. "Thank you...for keeping my attempted escape a secret."

He let out a weak cough and then winced, holding his sore shoulder. "Of course, Milady. I still long to keep you safe, even if you believe me to be a monster."

She shook her head. "You're not...a monster."

His eyes darkened with grief. "But I am. You know what I did. I killed Prince Tristan...your betrothed."

"I know," she whispered, avoiding his eyes, afraid it would give away her secret. Airell drew in a sharp breath and tears filled her eyes, but not for the reason she thought. She saw the pain and remorse in his eyes and wanted to relieve him of it, but she couldn't. If Prince Tiernay found out the truth, she could be putting the Órlaithan king and his surviving people in danger. So much of what Airell thought she knew about Prince Tiernay's character had been a lie. Now she couldn't trust him like before, although she *did* care about him deeply. The realization disturbed her, but she couldn't deny it.

His eyes gazed into hers in confusion. "Why are you helping me, Princess? I am your enemy. You could have let me die and been rid of me."

She looked into his hazel eyes for a moment, wondering why herself. Then she answered with the only truth she knew for certain. "'Tis the honorable thing to do."

"Thank you. I do not deserve your kindness." He shifted to sit up further on his pillow, wincing with the effort. When he met her gaze again, the intense look in his hazel eyes sent tingles down her spine. "I assume you realize by now, our marriage alliance was invalid."

"Aye," she answered with a trembling chin as a wave of betrayal washed over her again.

"I did not wish for this either, Milady. 'Twas not my choice. However, we must learn to live with this arrangement."

Airell nodded in agreement, heart breaking with the realization she had no other options.

He let out a deep sigh. "If you promise not to attempt another escape and play the part of my bride for the winter in Brannagh, I will make you a promise as well."

She looked up then and furrowed her brow. "What kind of promise?"

"I will do everything in my power to convince King Malcolm to annul our marriage and allow you return to Daireann. Even if he does not agree, I will help you escape. You have my word."

Airell stared at him and held her breath, unsure if her ears had deceived her. Yet the sincerity in the prince's eyes conveyed he spoke the truth.

With the hope of returning home to Dairiann and seeing her family again nestled in her heart, she agreed to his terms. For the winter she would pretend to be his happy bride.

The next five days at sea fell into a strange new routine for Tiernay. After the first night being cared for by Lady Airell in his old cabin, he resumed sleeping in the crew's quarters in a hammock, although his aching shoulder protested. While he usually loved life at sea, the last leg of the journey was torturous for him, but not only because of his injury.

Lady Airell tended to his shoulder every day, replacing the bandages and checking for swelling. They took their morning and evening walks on the deck as well, but it seemed like a chore for her now—only done for show. They did not speak as freely as before, either. It seemed it would take time to earn back her trust. She also spent an exorbitant amount of time teaching his servant, Slade, how to read, per their agreement. Isla, her new maid, even joined them. The girl kept a wary eye on him at all times, but didn't seem quite as terrified since he had saved Lady Airell from drowning. It seemed Isla had come to realize he didn't intend to harm any of them.

The temperature dipped lower each day they continued on a northerly course and on the fourth day, a gray coverlet rolled over the sky, muting the sun. Then a cold drizzle fell, eventually icing up the deck and making the simple task of walking treacherous for everyone. For the first few days, Lady Airell had ventured out of her cabin wrapped in furs to keep warm, but when the ice came, she remained inside.

Finally, on the morning of the sixth day at sea, the temperature plummeted even further, but as thick snow began to fall and gather on the deck, he saw the Dorcha Cliffs rising in the distance. His heart rumbled in his chest. They were nearly home.

CHAPTER FOURTEEN

Dark Passages

Approaching the shadowed cliffs, a chill tingled up Airell's spine, in spite of the furs wrapped tightly around her. The rock formations jutted out into the water in defiance, like dark fingers of death reaching toward her.

Then she breathed a sigh of relief when a large half-moon shaped harbor and majestic castle appeared out of the mist. Her eyes travelled over the lofty ramparts, arched terraces and open courtyards. Her heart thumped with joy, believing for the first time living in this strange land would not be so terrible after all. She looked forward to seeing the seals, puffins and gulls the prince had described.

After the ships were anchored, her happiness turned to confusion when Prince Tiernay helped her and Isla into a rowboat and tucked a few blankets around them before setting off. Then as the guards started rowing away from the ship, Airell craned her neck to watch the welcoming castle drift from her sight.

"The Solas Fortress has been abandoned, Milady," Prince Tiernay explained in a low voice. "The Dub Hach Fortress is heavily fortified and easier to protect. It will be another two hours' journey to the entrance."

She nodded as they followed King Malcolm's boat down a narrow canal, surrounded by steep jagged cliffs on each side and noticed several other vessels trailing behind them.

After what seemed like an eternity of navigating through the icy waters, a dark fortress appeared, jutting above the cliffs and slicing into the sky. A few minutes later at a curve in the waterway, they neared a hidden passageway blocked off by a heavy iron gate.

Her breath caught in her chest as the gate lifted with a grinding noise. The guards lit torches to light their way while navigating the dark waterways under the cliffs. The passageway branched off three different directions, but their boat followed the king's vessel down the one farthest to the right, journeying deeper and deeper into the darkness. The stale smell in the cave irritated her nose and the princess started to fear she would never see the light of day again.

"'Twill not be much longer, Milady."

Airell startled at Prince Tiernay's low voice echoing off the cavern's stone walls and offered a quick nod of understanding after calming herself. Then she clutched Isla's hand for comfort during the rest of the journey.

After a deep bend in the passage, they finally reached a large stone platform jutting out of the water and an arched tunnel opening, blocked off with another iron gate. Within seconds it was open and guards filed out of the tunnel, bowing before King Malcolm.

When Prince Tiernay helped her out of the boat, Airell had never been happier to be standing on solid ground. After the guards bowed before them, they followed the king down the tunnel lit with torches and emerged into a larger room looking more like a fortress. The ceilings grew higher as they walked and the walls were constructed of square cut stone like she was accustomed to in Daireann. They continued further down several hallways and the air smelled less stale than before.

Soon, Isla and Slade were instructed to wait outside with the servants before they entered a grand room with tapestries on the walls, regal engraved stone tiles on the floor and a platform with a large throne in the center and three smaller thrones on either side. It was still dark and much different from the throne room in Daireann, but somehow it brought her a small ounce of comfort after being in an underground cave for the last leg of their journey.

The king immediately took his throne and then two tall ladies appeared in the room, taking their places beside him. King Malcolm kissed the taller woman's hand and then motioned for Tiernay to come forward.

The prince gently touched Airell's back, guiding her toward the platform. Then he introduced her to his mother and sister. Airell offered a curtsy, feeling small in the presence of the royal family.

Tiernay's mother, Queen Ciara, had to be one of the most beautiful and regal women she'd ever met. Her long and silky chestnut hair, separated into two long braids adorned with golden beads reaching her waist and her purple gown was made of fine and ordinate brocade material, the train flowing down the back over the stone floor.

His sister, Fiona, was just as lovely, taking after her mother, only she stood a bit shorter and wore a simple black gown. Her eyes had dark circles underneath and she seemed listless, staring at her with a ghostly expression, her lips forming a straight line.

The king clapped his hands together and a regal smile spread across his face. "Now that you are all properly introduced, there will be a joyous feast tonight to celebrate this union."

Airell felt dizzy as she glanced in Prince Tiernay's direction. He didn't look at her, but she could see his jaw tense up in discomfort, obviously not ready to present her in public so soon.

A few moments later, a nobleman came in requesting the king's presence, leaving her with the prince, his mother and sister.

Queen Ciara's hazel eyes brightened as she descended from the throne with a smile, relaxing in the absence of the king. She approached them and hugged her son tight. A few tears clouded the queen's eyes before she released him. "You have grown into a man in your absence, my son. And now you have taken a bride. How wonderful." Her expression turned somber and her voice fell to a whisper. "We will talk in private soon. There is much to discuss."

Tiernay nodded and then Ciara turned to Airell, taking one of her hands and holding it for a moment. "Let me be the first to welcome you to our kingdom. 'Tis a privilege to have you as part of our family."

"Mine as well."

"Come, my dear. You must be weary from your long voyage. We will have the servants prepare my son's room to accommodate a lady and make sure you are comfortable as possible. It will have to do until we can prepare larger chambers suitable for a married couple. For now you can borrow my chambers and the servants will draw your bath and help you dress for tonight's celebration."

"Oh, thank you, Your Majesty, but I'd hate for you to fuss over me. I know you must have your own duties to look after."

"I insist," the queen announced with a flourish of her elegant hand. "How often does one get the privilege of meeting a new daughter-in-law and doting on her for the afternoon? I wish to know all about you. Come, we have little time and much to do."

As she followed the queen and princess out of the throne room, Airell caught Prince Tiernay's gaze one more time and a shudder passed through her body at the thought of being separated from him in the strange fortress.

Tiernay gave her a reassuring smile and nod of his head before she turned the corner, bringing her comfort and confusion at the same time. She had come to rely on him more than she wished. Now everything was changing again and she didn't know whether to be happy or dismayed.

Prince Tiernay knelt before his mother and hung his head, too ashamed to look into her eyes. In the months he had been away, he had done things—terrible things—and now she knew it all. He had dreaded this conversation all afternoon and now he had no choice but to see his mother's disappointment at his weakness.

"Tiernay," she whispered. When he finally looked up, her eyes weren't filled with disappointment, but compassion. "If you hadn't followed your uncle's orders, your sister and I would have met our end. No one should have to make that kind of decision. Ask God's forgiveness, my son. Release yourself from this heavy burden."

He closed his eyes and shook his head hard as a single tear escaped. "I'm a murderer...a monster. I do not deserve forgiveness. My soul is condemned forever now."

She lifted his chin and gazed into his eyes. "'Tis not true. I will never believe it. I have made compromises, too, that I regret every day. I have betrayed my own heart...in marrying your uncle and pretending to love him, when in my soul, I despise him for all the evil he has done. But soon we will escape this prison...and we will take your new bride with us. Start a new life somewhere in North Rhona with my people. My nephew, Ewan, will not turn us away." She paused and a smile graced her mouth for the first time since the beginning of their conversation. "Now, let us speak of more pleasant things. Your bride is an angel and I can tell you care for her a great deal."

He nodded miserably. "I do, but now that she knows what I have done, she will never learn to love me."

"Give it time, my beloved son. Matters of the heart are complicated indeed, but God has a way of working things out in time. And once we escape this fortress and find a refuge elsewhere, it will be easier for her to see the man you really are."

Tiernay agreed, but decided to keep his agreement with Lady Airell a secret from his mother for the time being. News of his marriage lifted her spirits and he didn't wish to ruin it with the knowledge his new wife would leave them in the springtime. He stood from the floor and then sat beside her on the long padded bench by the window. "Do you still believe our plan to escape the fortress will work?"

She nodded and her hazel eyes filled with hope. "Aye. We have all winter to gather supporters and perfect our plans."

He gripped his mother's hand, drawing strength from her quiet courage. "There is much to discuss. We need to share our plans with Fiona as well."

She patted his cheek with a smile. "Aye, but for now we have a wedding celebration to attend."

CHAPTER FIFTEEN

Wedding Feast

There were at least fifty guests at the celebration—mostly nobility who were close friends of the king and queen. There were also her new ladies-in-waiting, whom she hoped to become better acquainted with.

Looking around the table, she recognized the differences in Tiernay's kingdom from her own. In Daireann the women loved vibrant clothing matching the wildflowers on the rolling hills and cliffs by Loch Maorga. However, the women in Brannagh dressed in heavier fabrics and darker colors. She suddenly felt out of place in her silk, sky blue gown.

Everything seemed heavier and darker in this new kingdom. The guests carried on conversations, played games and seemed to be enjoying themselves, but they didn't dance and they didn't celebrate or laugh as joyfully as her kingdom did. A sudden wave of homesickness hit her unexpectedly. She felt Prince Tiernay's eyes on her, but avoided looking at him in fear she would burst into tears.

Airell managed to keep her emotions at bay for the remainder of the feast and even afterwards when her new maids helped her change into her nightgown and robe in the chambers she would share with her new husband. However, as soon as they left the room, lonely sobs shook her body. Airell remembered everything from the past few weeks and missed her family so much it made her double over. She could barely breathe while sitting on the bed and praying for God's help.

Tiernay took his time going to his chambers that night, stopping to socialize with a few nobles long after Lady Airell excused herself from the feast. It truth, he was nervous about how things would change between them now. It was one thing being in close quarters on the ship with the crew who didn't care much about their relationship or lack thereof, but now they were in a large fortress where everyone knew they were husband and wife. They were expected to look like a married couple.

When he finally did retire to his room, he found Lady Airell curled up in a ball on the bed, fast asleep with her back to him. He removed his cloak and hung it on a hook. Then he tiptoed across the room and leaned over to check on his new bride, smiling while brushing a few strands of golden hair away from her beautiful face.

His smile faded when she sniffled and her lips quivered in her sleep. Then he noticed her cheeks were bright pink and puffy from crying. The poor girl had been through so much in the recent weeks and was completely exhausted, physically and emotionally.

Letting out a sigh, he covered her with a blanket

and then paused for a moment to gaze at the delicate beauty of her face one more time. "Good night, my bride," he whispered and barely brushed her cheek with his lips, silently hoping he would become a man worthy of her love someday.

Then, quite weary himself, Tiernay gathered extra blankets and a pillow and arranged them on the floor as a makeshift bed. He drifted off to sleep almost as soon as his head rested on the pillow.

Airell awakened to the sound of Prince Tiernay stirring on the floor next to the hearth. She peeked at him through one eyelid and noticed his wince of pain before he carefully sat up, rubbed his sore shoulder and then rolled up his bedding. A pang of guilt shot through her, knowing she had overtaken his bed, leaving him to sleep on the floor.

She vaguely remembered him covering her with a blanket and kissing her cheek the night before. She had been half awake, but didn't open her eyes. His sweet words of affection had both surprised and warmed her heart, even though she still didn't know if she could trust him fully. It seemed he truly did care for her in some way.

She closed her one open eye as he looked in her direction while grabbing some fresh clothes. Then she heard him retreat to the other room to change. Airell pretended to be asleep until she heard the outer chamber door open and close.

Then she sat up and yawned before looking around the room, having not paid much attention the night before. The furnishings were luxurious, but masculine in nature with fur rugs on the floor. There was a small window, letting some light in, but it was too high for her to look out. However, she noticed a checkered board and hand-carved pieces shaped into kings, queens, knights and other figures on a shelf underneath it. The walls were covered with rich colored tapestries and walking across to the hearth, her toes sunk into the soft gray fur rug. She warmed herself by the fire, pleased to see Tiernay had added another log for her before leaving.

Airell pulled her robe tighter around herself and padded to the far room, seeing another door slightly cracked open. She peeked through, noticing a small sitting area with a table and wooden chairs around it. In the far corner she saw the prince's study, complete with a desk, armchair and several shelves full of books behind it. Her heart soared as she walked in, recognizing all kinds of familiar literature—philosophy, religious texts and even some poetry. Airell had always loved books and considered Tiernay's collection a rare treasure.

A moment later, a sudden knock on the door interrupted her moment of bliss. She rushed back to the sleeping chamber and sat on the bed, knowing it was most likely her maids. "You may enter," Airell called out and smiled when Isla came in with her breakfast on a tray.

"Good morning, Your Majesty." The young girl looked well rested and happy to see her.

"Oh, 'tis so good to see a familiar face. How did you sleep? Did they find you acceptable living quarters?"

She set the tray on her bed. "Aye, they have treated me well. I have maid's quarters just down the hall from you."

Airelle breathed a sigh of relief, glad Lady Isla's true status as a countess of Orlaith had been kept secret. She felt sorry for Isla, being treated below her station, but at least she was safe.

They spent several minutes talking after she finished breakfast and then another knock sounded on the door. Airell told them to come in, but wasn't prepared for the parade of people entering through her chamber door. Queen Ciara and Lady Fiona came in first, followed by several servants and two seamstresses. Soon they were taking her measurements and then another group of servants came in carrying large bolts of fabric.

The queen appeared in her element, ordering the servants to try different fabrics with the dress styles. "Oh, Tiernay would adore this royal blue. 'Tis his favorite color," she crooned and then tapped her chin when the servant held the heavy fabric up to Airell. The queen looked at her and smiled in approval. "Lovely. What do you think, my dear?"

Airell shrugged in a shy manner. "'Tis beautiful, but I must confess I am not familiar with the fashions in this kingdom. They are quite different from what I am used to. I will trust you to decide, Your Majesty." She turned to her new sister-in-law who sat on a wooden chair surrounded by fabrics in the corner of the room. "I would love to hear your opinions too, Lady Fiona."

The young woman flinched at the sound of her own name and dashed out of the room with a swish of her black skirt, looking ready to burst into tears.

Airell turned the queen with wide eyes. "Did I say the wrong thing? I hope I didn't offend the princess."

Queen Ciara shook her head, looking grieved. "She will return soon. It has nothing to do with what you said. My daughter hasn't spoken to anyone except me in months."

"I am sorry to hear that." Airell stared at the door Lady Fiona had fled from. What could have happened to traumatize the poor young woman and why did she wear mourning clothes? She would have to remember to pray for her.

Queen Ciara's sigh, brought Airell out of her tangled thoughts. "Well, we must get back to your fitting. You will need a completely new wardrobe to last through our cold winters." The queen smiled with a nod and continued choosing different colored bolts in shades of olive green, plum and burgundy. Airell had never seen so many fabrics in her life. It was true, she had a large closet full of gowns back home in Daireann, but had collected them gradually over the years, passing them down to Gwyn after growing out of them. She had never been fitted for an entire new wardrobe all at once. When they were finished, Lady Airell felt mentally drained, hungry for the midday meal and anxious to see Prince Tiernay, whom had been absent the entire morning.

Tiernay paced while waiting for the ladies to arrive at the midday meal in the great hall. When his mother, sister and Lady Airell appeared at the entrance, he stopped and stared for a moment. His new bride looked stunning in an elegant, burgundy brocade gown he recognized as one of his sister, Fiona's. It was a little long on her, but she still looked stunning, although a little uncomfortable in the heavy fabric. He took her hand and escorted her to their place at the long table in the middle of the room.

After they were settled, he struggled to think of

subjects to bring up in public. Finally he turned to her and asked how her morning went.

She offered a weary smile. "It was…busy, however I should have my new wardrobe for winter in a few weeks. Your mother and sister were kind enough to help me choose the styles and colors."

"Good, it gets cold in the fortress in the winter."

She took a sip of her drink and then shifted uncomfortably in her borrowed gown. "So I'm told. It's going to be an adjustment, but I will get used to it with time."

His eyebrows furrowed, remembering what his mother said about giving Airell time to grow closer to him and felt guilty for his absence earlier. "Is there anything I can do to make your adjustment to this new kingdom easier?"

She drummed her fingers on the table before glancing up with a shy expression. "I…I hope you don't mind, but I discovered the library in your study. Would you mind if I read some of your books?"

"Of course you may." He grinned and let out a light chuckle at the child-like joy in her eyes over a few shelves of dusty books she'd discovered. Tiernay couldn't resist lifting her delicate hand and kissing it. "Enjoy them. What is mine is now yours, my love."

Lady Airell flinched—barely enough for anyone else to notice, but *he* did and released her hand. The word *love* had slipped from his lips unexpectedly and now she avoided his eyes and her hand trembled while taking another drink from her goblet. "Thank you," she replied barely above a whisper.

Tiernay's heart sunk at her reaction. In truth, his spontaneous declaration had surprised him as well. He had been numb for so long, forced to bend to his uncle's will, but since meeting Lady Airell his emotions had awakened again. Did he really love her so soon—or had it been an act for the king and the rest of the court? Either way, he wished he could pluck the words out of the air, but it was too late. To his dismay, it seemed they were forever doomed to take one stride forward and two strides back.

CHAPTER SIXTEEN

Middle Ground

A tear dripped onto Airell's pillow as her chamber door clicked shut. For several weeks, Prince Tiernay had fallen into the habit of coming into their chambers late at night, long after her bedtime. He slept in his usual place on the floor and then snuck away before the dawn. Airell became increasingly anxious about their relationship. After the second meal they shared together at the fortress, she only talked with him in public. His mention of *love* had shocked her. She meant to talk with him and explain her reaction, but they were never alone long enough to have the conversation.

She quenched her loneliness by spending time getting to know the ladies-in-waiting and continuing to give Slade and Isla reading lessons in secret. When there was no one to talk to in the court, she spent an exorbitant amount of time reading Tiernay's books.

About half an hour after the prince left, a knock on the door made her jump. Airell sat up, wiped her moist cheeks and told them to come in, expecting it to be Isla serving her breakfast. However, she lurched in surprise, seeing the queen carrying in a tray almost overflowing with food.

She sat up and attempted to smooth her tangled hair to look halfway presentable. "Y-your Majesty! I-I apologize. I was not expecting you."

Queen Ciara offered a sweet smile, sat the tray next to her and then took a seat at the foot of the bed. "Do not fret, my daughter. It was I who came unannounced. Forgive me, but I have noticed you've barely touched your meals lately. I thought if I hand-delivered your breakfast, with a variety of choices, I might persuade you to eat. You have grown thin since arriving here in our kingdom."

Airell relaxed a little then, thankful Tiernay's mother had such a warm and nurturing spirit. In the absence of her own mother, it was comforting to have someone treat her like a daughter. She sampled some eggs and sipped on her juice to satisfy the queen. "Thank you, Your Majesty. All of the food served here is wonderful. I simply do not have much of an appetite."

Queen Ciara frowned and felt her forehead. "Are you ill, my dear? You seem flushed." Her voice lowered to a whisper. "Is is possible you could be...with child?"

"No, Your Majesty. 'Tis nothing like that. The prince and I...we barely even speak to each other."

Gentle understanding filled the elder woman's eyes and Airell's face contorted as the queen took her hand and gently patted the back of it. "Arranged marriages can be difficult, especially in the early days. When I first married Tiernay's father, we were both so young and timid around each other. We barely spoke for months, except in public. I thought I had done something to displease him, but he was simply shy—we both were."

Airell wiped her tears with her free hand and sniffled, knowing her relationship with Tiernay was more complex than simply being shy. His part in the fall of Órlaith disturbed her—the fact that he could act so gentle toward her, but yet so cruel to the innocent people of Órlaith, even to the point of attempting to murder their prince. Still, she did not wish to reveal her insecurities about Tiernay's past sins with his mother. It didn't feel right. Instead she decided to avoid the subject of the prince altogether. "How did you overcome your shyness around each other?"

Queen Ciara smiled with a nostalgic gleam in her eyes. "Eventually we began to learn things about each other and became friends...and after many years, our friendship blossomed into love." Then it was the queen's turn to wipe away a few tears.

"What happened to him?"

The queen pursed her lips for a moment before answering. "Ten years ago he became mysteriously ill. There was nothing the physicians could do for him." Her face turned stony and her voice fell to a whisper. "They said he'd been poisoned by one of our enemies, but I believe his brother was responsible."

Airell's eyes widened in shock and she kept her voice low. "King Malcolm poisoned his own brother? Why would he do such a terrible thing?"

The queen nodded, eyes flashing with anger and grief. "He'd been jealous of his elder brother since birth and when Donally married me, Malcolm became covetous and obsessed. My husband became fearful for his life and my own. He sent his brother away to live in this fortress to put space between them. But Prince Malcolm's reach was longer than he thought. He succeeded in murdering the king, taking me as his bride and stealing Tiernay's right to rule the kingdom. We are nothing but stolen possessions to him now—part of his treasure hoard—but expendable since I haven't been able to bear his child. Tierney is the closest thing he has to an heir and thus has become his slave."

Airell struggled to breathe while digesting everything Queen Ciara told her. Then all at once she understood. Tiernay always seemed so conflicted, like he despised himself for what he had done in Órlaith. She turned toward the queen, her cobalt eyes wide, seeing everything much clearer than before. "He did those terrible things for you and Lady Fiona…to keep you both safe."

The queen nodded. "Aye, my son's weakness has always been his love for us. 'Tis not in his nature to be cruel or foul-tempered. Whatever darkness you have seen in him has been caused by his uncle. He is trying to corrupt him and we cannot allow it happen. You see, Tiernay is our kingdom's future and our only hope to escape the tyranny of King Malcolm." Queen Ciara paused and wiped a tear from her cheek before continuing. "My son believes his soul is condemned because of the sins he committed in Órlaith. He feels unworthy to claim his rightful place on the throne. Tiernay needs our encouragement to become the king God always intended for him to be."

Airell nodded and something shifted in her heart—something she didn't expect. "How can I help?"

Tiernay entered his chambers late in the night like usual and threw another log onto the dying fire in the hearth. Then he rolled out his bedding and pillow for another uncomfortable night's sleep on the floor. He had barely closed his eyes when he heard Lady Airell stirring on the bed. In the dim firelight he could tell her eyes were open and gazing in his direction. He turned onto his side, propping himself halfway up with his elbow as concern furrowed his brow. "Milady, is something troubling you?"

"I cannot sleep."

He started to rise. "Are you chilled? I could fetch another blanket for you."

She shook her head. "No, I am comfortable. Thank you." She remained silent for a while and he rested his head back on the pillow as they continued studying each other. When she spoke again, her voice sounded grieved. "Have I displeased you in some way, Milord?"

He sat completely up now, heart twisting at the hurt in her voice. "Of course not, Lady Airell. How could I ever be displeased with you?"

She sat up, letting her stocking-covered feet hang over the side of the bed, but dropped her gaze from him. "We used to take walks together on the ship. Now we barely spend any time in each other's company. I know it is partially my doing."

"'Tis not your fault, Milady."

"Airell," she corrected. "When we're alone, please just call me Airell. We are supposed to be acting like husband and wife after all."

"Very well, *Airell*," he replied with a grin. A dark cloud had hung over his head for several weeks, but with a few sweet words, she'd managed to lift it. "But on one condition," he continued. "You must call me Tiernay."

She looked back up at him and smiled as the faint golden light from the fire danced across her lovely face. "Very well. I accept your condition, *Tiernay*."

He chuckled, enjoying the way his name sounded on her lips. "So, do you wish to sit by the hearth and talk for a while?"

She glanced at his handcrafted game on the shelf under the window and then back at him. "I think I have a better idea."

CHAPTER SEVENTEEN

Visitors

Reagan breathed a sigh of relief after finding her husband standing in the courtyard. He looked over Beatha Valley which was now covered in a thick layer of snow. "There you are, my love. I have searched the entire castle from top to bottom."

Arlan turned to her with a sad smile, his face pale and gaunt. "I apologize for worrying you. I couldn't remain inside any longer." After taking his hand in hers, he looked back at the valley in silence.

A faint rattle deep in his lungs reminded her he had not been the same since the siege on their kingdom. The cold air wasn't good for him at all. She needed to find out why he had come outside and then convince him to come in.

"Is something troubling you?" she tried.

He let out a deep exhausted sigh. "Somehow I still believe one day my sister will return. She does not belong in the northern kingdom as King Malcolm's prisoner. 'Tis my fault."

She rested her head against his shoulder and clung to his arm. Reagan wanted to tell him about her secret message to South Rhona, requesting aid. However, after weeks of no response, she didn't want to get his hopes up. "Arlan, please don't blame yourself. I was riddled with guilt at first as well, but then I realized Airell would have found a way to do this, even if we had known her plan and tried to stop her. She is just as stubborn as her brother."

He choked out a weak laugh before kissing her cheek and resting his head against her auburn hair. "True."

"Everything will be fine, my love. Your sister is tougher than she seems."

"I know." The rattle in his lungs grew louder and Arlan pulled out his handkerchief before sputtering out several coughs. A moment later he began hacking violently and Reagan noticed speckles of crimson blood on the cloth in his hand.

"Arlan!" she wrapped her arm around his waist and guided him toward the castle entrance. "Come, we must get you back to bed."

After making sure Arlan was comfortable, Reagan left the queen mother and Gwyn in the royal chambers to sit with him and followed the physician into the hallway. "How bad is it?" she asked after closing the chamber door behind them.

The physician busied himself putting one last instrument in his bag. When he looked up, his grieved expression filled her heart with fear. "The sickness in his lungs is worsening. I've given him herbs to soothe his lungs, but we must limit his stress and make sure he gets plenty of rest. Only time will tell if he will overcome his illness."

After thanking the doctor, Reagan walked back into the room as numbness settled over her. "The physician is hopeful the herbs will help," she told Queen Norah and Lady Gwyneth after they looked at her with questioning eyes. Guilt filled her when relieved expressions spread across their faces, knowing she had told them a half-truth, but she couldn't accept the grim reality of their situation yet—couldn't say it out loud.

It wasn't until Arlan's mother and sister left the room to let him rest that Reagan could admit her own fears. She sat beside Arlan on the bed, watching him sleep. Then she took his hand and kissed it, willing him to recover and become strong and healthy again. Letting out a deep sigh, she rested her head on the pillow beside him, never letting go of his hand. "You have to fight this, Arlan. I need you to stay with me." She paused as a tear dripped down her cheek. "I...I need you."

His eyelids fluttered open and a weak smile formed on his lips. "I'm still here, my love." He let out a few raspy breaths before speaking again. "You needn't worry. Everything will be fine."

She smiled for Arlan's sake and ran her fingers over his cheek. "I know. Everything seems better when I look into your eyes." Reagan leaned forward and kissed his forehead. "I apologize for waking you. Go back to sleep, my love."

He closed his eyes and eventually fell asleep again. He looked so peaceful Reagan started drifting off with him, but a knock on the door jolted her awake. She slipped off the bed and walked out the door, careful not to disturb her husband.

After the door clicked shut, the servant bowed. "I apologize, Your Majesty. The military commander requests your presence on the ramparts. A company of men are approaching from the east."

Reagan's heart pounded so hard, she could barely hear the rest of what the servant told her. "I'll be right there," she said breathlessly and rushed back into the room to grab her bow and arrows. If this was another attack on the castle, she refused to be left defenseless.

After traveling for weeks through the treacherous snow-covered mountains, King Tristan managed a weary smile as Beatha Castle came into view. It was the most beautiful sight he'd witnessed in a long time. The walls were still standing, which meant his betrothed was safe within them.

When they reached the gates, a woman's voice stopped him in his tracks. "What is your business here?"

He looked up and saw a group of archers on the ramparts. An auburn-haired archeress stood in the center, holding an arrow back on the string of her bow, aimed at his chest. "We come in peace, Milady. I am King Tristan, from the Kingdom of Órlaith. I have come with my cousin, Leland, the Earl of Kiely, to speak with King Arlan."

The archeress kept her bow raised and her eyes narrowed. "We have heard *Prince* Tristan died in battle."

He nodded. "I nearly did. My people have sought refuge in Kiely. If you need further confirmation, send someone out to confirm my ring bears the royal crest."

The archeress relaxed and lowered her bow, finally looking past his rugged appearance and recognizing he spoke the truth. "'Tis not necessary. Open the gates," she ordered.

Within a few minutes, King Tristan and his company were gathered inside the courtyard and proper introductions were made. He discovered the red-haired archeress was Queen Reagan. He bowed before her and then asked about the king.

Her expression turned somber. "I know you traveled all this way, but I am afraid speaking with the king will have to wait at least a few days."

"Could he not spare a few minutes? The matter is of most urgency."

Queen Reagan's green eyes bored into his and she crossed her arms. "I apologize, Milord. The king is very ill and cannot be bothered with business matters at the moment. I am acting as regent. Anything you need to talk with him about will have to go through me."

He sighed and crossed his arms in frustration. "I am gathering an army to defeat King Malcolm and his forces in the north. I had hoped King Arlan would support my quest."

Lady Reagan shook her head. "Our army is depleted, Milord. Our remaining soldiers must stay here to protect from further attack."

"Then I will go to the surrounding villages. If I could only talk to the king for a moment. Even a small company of soldiers would help greatly."

She shook her head. "No. I cannot allow it at this time. Perhaps in a few months."

The king looked down and gritted his teeth at the woman's stubbornness. Had his long journey been for naught? Had he only come all this way to be humiliated? He reined in his temper and glanced back up with one last ounce of hope. "And what of Lady Airell? May

I speak with her?"

Tears filled the queen's eyes and his heart sunk. "I must apologize again, Milord. Lady Airell has married the northern prince to make a peace alliance."

Tristan's heart twisted in a combination of rage, grief and utter despair, thinking of Lady Airell being kept prisoner by the Dark Lord of the north. He couldn't afford to wait until spring to gather an army—not when she needed him. He had made a promise to King Fallon to keep her safe. Somehow he had to find a way to honor his promise, even if it meant going against Lady Reagan.

CHAPTER EIGHTEEN

Winter Games

"Checkmate," Airell declared and then looked up at him with a shy grin. "Wait, did you let me win?"

Tiernay smiled at her in the dim light from the window and chuckled in amusement. "I did nothing of the sort, Milady."

"Airell," she corrected with a raised eyebrow, gently reminding him of their agreement to use first names while not in public.

"*Airell*," he repeated softly and something about the subtle affection in his tone created the sensation of butterflies fluttering around in her stomach. "Truly, your chess skills have grown rapidly in only a few days. I'm impressed."

She looked down to hide her blush and started setting up the game board again. Now that they had finally broken the ice since arriving at the fortress, Airell had started to feel quite happy and content around him in spite of the circumstances. She enjoyed his company a little more each day. "Thank you." Her eyes twinkled as pleasant memories came to her. "I used to play games with my younger sister, Gwyn, all the time. She loves new games and I'm sure she would love this one. If I still lived in our kingdom we would most likely play it over and over, neglecting sleep." Her smile faded as a wave of homesickness overcame her.

Tiernay seemed to recognize her change in mood and gave her a knowing look. "I am sure you miss your family."

She sniffled and tried to hold back her tears. "Aye. My siblings are very dear to me. Arlan, is very protective of my sister and I. We look up to him so much. I pray he still lives."

He placed his hand over hers on the table. "We have to hold out hope. I still plan to do everything in my power to make sure you see your family again. I know the anguish of being separated from those you love and wouldn't wish it on anyone. My sister wept so bitterly when I left...sometimes I wonder if she has forgiven me. 'Tis hard to tell since she no longer speaks to anyone. Fiona wasn't always like that. She used to be so joyful and carefree when we were children. 'Tis a shame."

"What changed her?"

Tiernay took one of his chess pieces and turned it over in his hand to study it. "My uncle forced her to marry a powerful lord from a southern part of our kingdom in exchange for help from his military." He gritted his teeth. "He was heartless and cruel toward my sister, but the marriage was short-lived. Her husband was slain in an uprising and Fiona returned to us about a month before I left for Órlaith, but she has never been the same."

Airell thought back to her confusion about Lady

Fiona's mourning clothes and timid behavior, but now she understood. "I'm sorry, Tiernay. I cannot imagine what she must have gone through. I will try harder to befriend her in the coming weeks. Perhaps she needs some gentle reassuring she is safe now."

Tiernay nodded. "Aye, but *is* she safe, Airell? Is *anyone* safe in this fortress with a mad king prowling the halls?" He shook his head with regret, seeing her alarmed expression and spoke softer. "I apologize if my blunt words frighten you. I simply do not want any of my loved ones to have a false sense of security within these walls. We must all be on our guard, but rest assured I would give my life before allowing any harm to come to you."

Airell managed a trembling smile and took Tiernay's hand in hers, heart aching at the thought. "I pray it never comes to that."

He sighed and gripped her hand tighter. "I grow weary of the stale air in this fortress. Would you like to come with me, Airell? There is something I'd like you to see."

Her blue eyes filled with excitement. "Anything to obtain some fresh air."

After bundling up in a warm fur cloak, mittens and hat, she allowed Tiernay to escort her through a foreign maze of hallways she had yet to explore. After several minutes, they reached a stone staircase spiraling up a tower. When they reached the top, Tiernay opened a heavy wooden door. The blast of cold air shocked her at first, but after they went out onto the ramparts, the sight took her breath away. Everything below was covered in a thick white blanket of snow, shimmering in the sunlight. The mist rose over the cliffs in a majestic cloud, forming rainbows where the light hit it just right.

"Oh, 'tis a breathtaking view!" Airell exclaimed, her mitten-covered fingers curling over the stone wall as she breathed in the fresh air. The cold stung her eyes and nose, but it exhilarated her to be outside after so many weeks confined in the fortress.

"I thought you would enjoy it. 'Tis my favorite place to think."

"Thank you. It brings back pleasant childhood memories. Gwyn and I used to enjoy walking through the courtyard after the first snow. She always managed to hit me with snowballs when I least expected it."

Tiernay chuckled from beside her. "Oh, she did?"

"Aye." She smiled while gazing out over the ramparts, deep in thought. A moment later an icy ball hit her lightly on the shoulder with a faint whoosh. She looked over in surprise, seeing the mischievous grin on the prince's face. Airell brushed the white powder off her shoulder and laughed while grabbing a handful of snow and tossing it back at him.

After that, a spontaneous game ensued with joyous giggles and white powder filling the air. They both dodged and ducked each other's throws until Airell slipped on the snow and found herself suspended in Tiernay's arms, his hazel eyes gazing into hers.

She held her breath for a moment before finding her words again. "Thank you for catching me, Milord."

He swept a few strands of snow-caked hair from her face and grinned, leaning closer. "*Tiernay*," he whispered and their lips almost met.

"Your Majesty," someone called out from behind, ending the moment abruptly.

Tiernay helped Airell stand and then turned toward the young servant with a stern expression. "What is it?"

He bowed. "I apologize for the intrusion, but King

Malcolm requests your presence in the treasure chamber."

An icy chill tingled up Tiernay's spine as one of his servants steered the rowboat down the watery passageway. At a sudden splash, he held his torch higher to see further down the cavern. Groups of bats hung from the craggy ceiling above and jagged stalactite pillars dripped with moisture. He relaxed—reasoning one of the pillars had broken off and landed in the water. Tiernay had never liked navigating the dark caverns beneath the fortress. The stale air and eternal darkness sent a foreboding feeling through him, but his uncle had spent an exorbitant amount of time counting his treasure the past few weeks. It had become the only place to speak with him.

Instead of dwelling on the darkness, the prince's thoughts turned back to the afternoon he'd spent with Airell. He saw her golden hair covered in white powder and the way she smiled at him right before they almost shared a kiss. A smile tingled on his lips, encouraged by the direction their relationship was heading. Did he dare to dream she might decide to stay with him after their escape?

When they arrived at the entrance to the king's secret chambers and stepped out of the boat, Tiernay grew uneasy again. However, after using his torch to travel down a series of narrow passages, he finally emerged into the large treasure chamber. There, he found his uncle dressed in his finest floor-length fur robe and golden jeweled crown, walking among his hoard of gold coins and chests full of rare jewels.

When King Malcolm looked up, the prince shuddered at the covetous gleam in his dark brooding eyes. Tiernay knew the haunting look well. After weeks of calm—content in his victories, the king was now hungry again—hungry for more death, destruction and the treasure that followed.

The prince swallowed his nerves and bowed. "You requested my presence, Uncle?"

For a moment, the king's eyes cleared and he fiddled with the golden rings on his fingers. "Nephew, it pleases me to see you. We must begin planning for the spring."

Tiernay furrowed his brow. "The spring, Your Majesty?"

"Aye," the king replied with a flourish of his robe and approached him, placing two large hands on Tiernay's shoulders. "Our kingdom is growing in strength. Soon we will be the greatest empire in the history of Ardena." His eyes flashed with a strange combination of pride and madness. "We will unite all the kingdoms into one and in the future it will all be yours. Órlaith and Daireann have bended in submission and now North and South Rhona are the only remaining obstacles standing in our way. Lord Caerul has sent messengers saying they have treasure in North and South Rhona—more gold than you can imagine."

Tiernay shook his head and motioned toward the rolling mounds of gold surrounding them. "Uncle, do we not have enough already?"

His uncle gritted his teeth and glanced to the side, surveying his hoard with hungry eyes. "'Tis never enough!" He let go of Tiernay and staggered back to the piles of gold, pausing to bend down and sift some through is fingers. "You are too much like your father—weak—but I long to make you strong," he growled. "Because of *my* generosity, you now possess the greatest treasure of Daireann and yet you still do not understand!" He clenched a tangle of pearl necklaces in his fist. "When you want something you must take it, or someone else will!"

Tiernay seethed beneath the surface, realizing he spoke of Princess Airell. His heart thundered in his chest, wanting to scream. She was not his possession, nor part of the spoils of a war he never wished to fight. Yet, he stayed silent, knowing his anger would accomplish nothing. He attempted to keep his voice low and calm. "Uncle, I realize having the gold from Rhona would increase our power, but wouldn't an alliance with them be worth even more?"

The king whipped around to look at him, eyes smoldering with rage, but after a moment he calmed and appeared to be considering his proposal. "You have given me much to think over, nephew. Perhaps your council will be useful to me after all." His uncle grimaced and massaged his temples before waving his nephew away dismissively. "You may go now."

Tiernay released a sudden puff of air, unaware he had been holding his breath, but still couldn't manage to relax as he left. Something about the way his uncle spoke so calm and almost coherent concerned him more than his rage. He was formulating a new plan and Tiernay had a feeling it was something sinister as usual.

CHAPTER NINETEEN

A Humbled King

Reagan tried her best to accommodate their royal guests, but she could tell King Tristan grew more anxious each day he waited to speak with Arlan. However, the physician's words about limiting her husband's stress remained forefront in her mind. Besides, the Órlaithan king would have to wait until the spring to travel north if he had any sense at all.

Still, as several days passed with no improvement, Arlan became more anxious, regardless of the fact he didn't know about their unexpected visitors. He talked about his sister more and more with the knowledge her birthday approached. He was still full of regret he hadn't been able to protect her. By the end of the week he'd started refusing even the broth she offered.

Reagan placed the bowl on a nearby tray and let out a sigh of despair. She had to find a way to keep him fighting and perhaps King Tristan was the key. She took his hand in hers and gazed into his cobalt eyes. "You must eat to keep your strength up, my love."

He coughed and rested his head back against his pillows. "I will, just let me rest for a spell."

Reagan nodded and brushed her fingers over his pale cheek. She debated with herself for a while before finally deciding to tell him the truth. "We have royal visitors this week. 'Tis King Tristan and his company. He wishes to speak with you."

Arlan's eyes flew open and he tried to sit up. "King Tristan? He lives...and he's here in Daireann? Reagan, why did you not tell me sooner?"

She placed her hand on his shoulder, keeping him from getting up. "I wanted to reduce your stress and wait until you felt better."

He fell back against his pillows, coughing into his handkerchief again. "You must send him in."

Reagan took his hand, trying to calm him. "Arlan...please don't strain yourself. I will do as you wish, but you have to do something for me first."

His breathing slowed and he stared at her in confusion. "What?"

She smiled as hope filled her heart, seeing the life return to his blue eyes. "You must drink the broth before I help you get ready. After all, the King of Daireann must look his best."

He chuckled softly at her stubborn nature. "Very well, pass it this way."

During the first few days at the fortress, King Tristan spent much of his time brooding over the delay in meeting with the Daireann King.

First, he paced the halls to release his anxiety, but then he found the armory. It was a large rectangular room in the lower level of the castle with weapons and armor stored along the outside walls, leaving the middle of the room for weapon practice. Tristan's mission to defeat King Malcolm and his nephew to save Princess Airell seemed to fuel his strength and he worked on rebuilding his archery and sword fighting skills. The first few days he took things slow. However, soon he felt ready to spar with a partner. His cousin, Leland, agreed but Tristan could tell he took it easy on him.

"Come now," he urged while easily deflecting one of Leland's swings. "At least make it a challenge for me."

His cousin sighed and then took a beginning stance again. "Very well."

The fight started out well until his cousin made a quick advance and Tristan deflected with a high arching swing. Something pulled in his chest and he cried out, dropping his sword and doubling over in pain.

Leland was at his side almost instantly, helping to steady him. "I believe that is enough for today. Wouldn't you agree?"

Tristan gasped for breath and nodded. "Aye. You may be right."

Ten minutes later, he was back in his chambers to change into fresh clothes. After pulling a new tunic over his head, he caught sight of his reflection in the mirror and stopped. He noticed the ugly scar through the neck opening in his unlaced tunic first, but then Tristan's eyes traveled upward. His golden hair and beard had grown long and scraggly—much different than his clean shaven and tidy appearance before the attack on Órlaith. What struck him most was the hollow, lifeless expression in his green eyes.

Seeing himself clearly for the first time in months, Tristan questioned his motivation for journeying to

Daireann and for a fleeting moment thought of returning to Kiely without even speaking to the king.

Now he realized the truth. The battle in Órlaith and his duel with Prince Tiernay on the cliff had not only scarred him physically, but his mind and heart had been poisoned with the thirst for revenge. He bore little resemblance to the prince he used to be—a prince with dreams of a bright future for his kingdom. Now he had inherited the Órlaithan throne, yet all he saw in the mirror was a broken man—a humbled king with no kingdom—only crumbled walls, death and ash.

A sudden knock on the door made Tristan lurch forward. He braced his hands against the dresser for a moment until his heartbeat slowed. "Come in," he rasped.

The door creaked open and a servant bowed before him. "Your Majesty, King Arlan requests your presence in his chambers."

When Tristan approached the royal chambers, Queen Reagan waited outside the door, green eyes boring into him like razor-sharp arrowheads. "The king has agreed to see you…and despite my reservations at first, I have decided to allow it."

Heat tingled up his spine, but he reined in his temper and gave a slight bow. "Thank you, Your Majesty."

She nodded. "Aye, but I must warn you, he is very weak. He must not endure any stress, or the meeting will end abruptly."

He agreed and allowed the queen to lead him into the royal chambers. All at once his irritation toward her for postponing their meeting evaporated away. The king sat propped up in bed with pillows. His blond hair looked well-groomed under his crown and he had an emerald green robe draped over his shoulders. However, the pallor shade of Arlan's face and lips gave away his condition.

Tristan bowed in respect. "Thank you for agreeing to see me, Your Majesty."

King Arlan smiled—blue eyes tired with dark circles underneath, but intense at the same time. "'Tis I who should be thanking you. In truth, I had begun to give up hope of being reunited with my sister. Thanks to you, it has been restored."

Tristan started to speak, but paused as Queen Reagan took a seat in the chair next to her husband and held his hand. He became acutely aware of her eyes on him and couldn't decide if he was more intimidated when she pointed an arrow at his chest or when she simply stared in his direction with those intense, suspicious green eyes. Could she know of his conflicted motivations for traveling to Brannagh?

He paused for a moment to take a breath and choose his words carefully. "I wish to go on a quest to rescue Princess Airell, from Brannagh. However, with my kingdom's military and resources depleted, I will need your aid."

The king's smile faded, but the determined look in his blue eyes remained. "Aye, you have my support. Our military is depleted as well, but I will send out messengers to the villages and our allies in South Rhona." He paused as a few deep ragged coughs tumbled out of his mouth, before continuing in a gravelly voice. "With God's help, by spring we should have an army large enough for the quest."

Spring. Tristan's heart lurched with the thought of waiting all winter, but deep down, knowing it was for the best, he agreed. At least he would have time to regain his full strength. Then, perhaps he would finally rid the world of the darkness in the north.

CHAPTER TWENTY

Revelations

Lady Airell's new wardrobe arrived right on time for her birthday celebration. She protested the event at first, but Tiernay convinced her it was a good way to meet more of the ladies and lords from around the kingdom. The new burgundy gown her maids helped her change into for the occasion was heavier than Airell was accustomed to, but she reasoned it would keep her warmer in the chilly fortress.

Other things had changed, too. Airell and Tiernay had moved into their new larger chambers. They both had their own studies and sitting rooms connecting to a bedroom chamber with a large luxurious four poster bed in the middle. However, Tiernay had given the bed to her and converted his sitting room into a small sleeping quarters for himself, complete with a small cot he could hide away in a wardrobe every morning.

Still, even though they were separated by a door for sleeping now, they continued talking and playing games by the fire late into the night.

After Isla finished arranging Airell's hair for the evening, a knock from the adjoining room made a smile spread across her face. "Come in. I am almost ready."

The prince opened the door and studied her for a moment while she put on some earrings "You look stunning," he said finally and cleared his throat.

"Thank you." Airell turned away to grab her cloak, trying to hide her blush. Her outfit choice hadn't seemed quite right until he complimented it. Now Airell knew she hadn't imagined it. Something had changed between them since the almost kiss in the snow. After regaining her composure, she turned and tucked her hand into the crook of his preferred arm and then he escorted her down to the great hall.

The feast was different this time, now that she knew most of the nobles. They stood in groups and talked for a while, although Airell's eyes searched for Tiernay several times before dinner and he appeared to be looking for her as well. Whenever they met each other's gaze, his smile filled her stomach with butterflies.

After dinner, Tiernay lingered beside her at the table, even after everyone else got up for more socializing. He lifted her hand and kissed it. "I have a surprise for you."

She stared at him in wonder. "A surprise? Isn't this grand party enough?"

He shook his head as instruments started playing. "'Tis only a small surprise." He stood up and gave a slight bow. "Would you care to dance, Milady?"

Airell stared at him in disbelief and then looked around nervously. "Will the king allow it?"

"Aye, my uncle has never said we cannot dance. We simply haven't had a reason to be merry in a long time."

"Very well then," Airell agreed, gulping down her nerves as Tiernay led her to the center of the room. He bowed and she curtsied. Then they rotated in a circle one direction and then the other, palm to palm before he gently lifted her by the waist. Airell's heart pounded as he put her feet back on the ground and continued the steps of the dance.

She'd barely had a chance to catch her breath before others were joining in. Then with a quick switch in partners, Tiernay rotated away from her and she lost him in the crowd. However, his absence was brief and soon enough, he reappeared through a whirlwind of flowing fabrics and other dancers. She smiled and breathed a sigh of relief as they rotated together palm to palm again. Before long she was paired with someone else, but at the end of the dance they were face to face. His hazel eyes gazed into hers, making her heart flutter. What were these strange new emotions sneaking up on her? She had learned to enjoy the prince's company over the last few months and he had earned back her trust, but these new feelings toward him confused her.

Airell recalled the pure joy and happiness in her heart when she had decided to accept Prince Tristan's proposal. Now the feelings she had developed toward Tiernay were just as pure, but deeper somehow.

Lady Airell was still attempting to sift through her new revelation when Queen Ciara pulled her into a circle dance. Over a dozen ladies joined in, hands linked together and rotating one way, while the men rotated in a similar circle nearby.

Everyone seemed to be having a merry time, except for Lady Fiona who huddled in a corner of the room by herself. Airell noticed her emerald gown right away—a stark difference from the black mourning clothes she had grown accustomed to her sister-in-law wearing. However, in spite of her bright colored gown, she appeared more troubled than usual. Her face looked pale and her eyes were red.

During another rotation, she noticed Tiernay break from the dance and approach his sister. He gently extended his hand, seeming to ask her something. Fiona fled the room and the prince went after her. By the time they reached the hall, Airell had left the dance and caught up.

"Fiona!" he called out as a flash of emerald fabric disappeared around the corner. He turned toward Airell with a grieved expression on his handsome face. "I simply asked her to dance." He shook his head and a faint tremble spread across his lips. "I'm at a loss, Airell. How can I earn back her trust? We used to be so close."

She gripped his hand and kissed it—an act that surprised them both, but it wasn't the time to discuss it. "Do not despair, Tiernay. I will try to talk with her alone this time."

He nodded, but clung to her fingers like he didn't want her to go. "Airell...I..." She stared into his misty hazel eyes for a moment, waiting for him to continue, but instead he slid his fingers from hers and managed a smile. "I'll speak with you later tonight...over a game of chess."

"Aye," she agreed, forcing herself to turn away.

When Airell arrived at Lady Fiona's chambers, she knocked and called to her first through the small crack in the door. There was no answer, so she stepped inside. "Lady Fiona, 'tis only Airell. I wanted to check on you." She heard a gagging noise and after stepping around the bed, she found Tiernay's sister on the floor leaning over her chamber pot. "Oh, Fiona. Are you all right?"

The princess looked up with a pale face and startled expression. Then she waved her away. "I'm fine. I wish to be alone."

Airell eased herself onto the floor next to Fiona and gently touched her back. "I could help." The young woman flinched at her touch and she withdrew her hand. "I'm sorry. I didn't mean to frighten you."

Fiona took a deep breath and leaned against the bed frame. "'Tis not your fault. I prefer not to be touched, but you did not know that."

"Can I fetch your maid to bring you something to ease your stomach or get a physician?"

She shook her head. "No, the sickness has passed. I'll be fine now." Fiona attempted to get up, but collapsed back to the floor, breathing hard while leaning her head against the bed. "I suppose I have dishonored my family once again with my weakness. Did my brother send you?"

Airell shook her head. "'Twas my choice. Fiona, your brother is only concerned about you. He believes you to be angry with him for leaving."

Fiona hung her head, shoulders trembling in the dim firelight. "'Tis not true. I could never be angry with Tiernay for trying to protect us. I simply cannot overcome this guilt in my own heart…knowing what our uncle forced him to do to keep us from harm. How can I look him in the eyes now?"

"He loves you, Fiona. 'Tis not your fault for your uncle's actions. Tiernay made his own choices and I'm sure he would do it again to keep your family protected and together."

Fiona shook her head, sobbing now. "But, don't you see? 'Twas all for naught."

"Why?"

Tiernay's sister wiped her eyes and glanced in her direction. "My uncle told me this morning that my days of mourning are over. He plans to forge an alliance with South Rhona. I am to wed Lord Fergus."

Airell's breathing changed to short ragged gasps at Fiona's words. "Queen Reagan would never allow it. Not against your will."

"She may be forced to. During times of war one must make sacrifices."

"Not if Tiernay and I can prevent it. We're leaving this place come spring. We will be free. Your brother has a plan."

"Aye," Fiona agreed, but her face looked grieved and pale. "But there is one thing he remains unaware of…something I have kept from everyone because it's dangerous for all of us. In the spring I will be unfit to travel."

Airell stared at her new sister-in-law as realization finally hit her. "Lady Fiona, are you with child?"

She nodded miserably while running a hand over the slight curve on her abdomen. Airell had never even noticed until then because she was so thin. "Aye, I've known since just before my husband's death…and it is becoming increasingly difficult to hide. If King Malcolm finds out and it ruins the alliance with Rhona, he will surely find a way to murder me, along with my unborn child. He doesn't need another heir to the Brannaghan throne around the fortress, disrupting his plans."

After praying for wisdom, Airell gripped her sister-in-law's hand, making her flinch at first, but then she squeezed her fingers in return, appearing desperate for help. "Fiona, your brother and I will never allow harm to come to you, or your child. I promise. But there is something we must do."

Fiona's tear filled hazel eyes filled with confusion. "What?"

"We must tell Tiernay and your mother without delay. This news will change things."

Prince Tiernay paced before the hearth in his mother's chambers, the weight of Fiona's confession crushing him with each step. Now everything made sense, but the truth was brutal and deadly. It seemed to poison the air in the room—suffocating him.

"I'm sorry, brother. I'm sorry for the hardship I have brought upon us all," his sister's frail voice whispered from across the room.

The sorrow in her tone made him stop and he crossed the room, gently pulling Fiona into his arms even though she resisted at first and then trembled against him. "You have nothing to apologize for, my sweet sister. You have proven braver than any of us, for you have bore this secret alone for so long."

After a moment, her stiff body relaxed and she began to sob against him. Tears rolled down Tiernay's cheeks as well. However, they were not tears of despair, but instead, tears of relief. His sister hadn't been angry with him after all. She had been acting out of unfounded guilt all this time, but now the misunderstanding had been resolved. Soon his mother joined in the hug and they wept together as a family, happy to be reunited once again.

When he looked up and wiped his eyes, Tiernay noticed Airell standing a few feet away, wiping tears of her
own. He extended his hand to her and when she approached, he enveloped her smaller delicate one in his
and kissed it. "Thank you, Airell. If not for you, my
family would still be divided."

"You have a treasure for a wife, my son. She has
united us and now we are stronger than ever." His
mother gripped his other hand and soon all four of
them joined in a circle.

Tiernay nodded as hope filled his heart once again.
"Aye. Now we must find supporters to help. There
have to be some in the kingdom who remain loyal to
father. I must ask them to pledge their loyalty to me."
He let out a tired sigh. "If only it did not seem like an
impossible task."

"They will, my son. King Malcolm is strong and
cruel. He forces the people into submission, but you
will never be that way. You have a true, kind and brave
heart like your father—the heart of a true king of
Brannagh. When the people see what I see in you, they
will not hesitate to follow you." Airell and Fiona nodded in agreement with his mother.

Tiernay swallowed his emotions. "I will try my best
to become a king Father would be proud of."

His mother smiled at him. "He would already be
proud."

He broke the circle and turned away to wipe the
tears gathering in his eyes. Tiernay stared at the glowing
embers in the hearth, unsure if he could live up to their
expectations, but longing with all his heart to try.
"Now, we must devise a new plan. Escaping on foot is
no longer an option with Fiona ready to give birth in
the spring. We must ask ourselves, what is the strength

of the king's military?"

"His numbers," his mother offered.

He nodded. "Aye, but loyalties can be swayed, like you said before. What else does he have?"

"Ships," Airell answered from beside him. "They are far superior to any of the kingdoms in Ardena. He caught Daireann by complete surprise. If his military had come by land, our messengers would have had sufficient time to warn us."

"Aye," he agreed, continuing to stare at the flames as an idea formed in his mind. "If we destroy most of the ships, saving only a few for us to escape, his power over us will be greatly reduced. It will take him over a month to pursue us through the snowy mountains to North Rhona and by that time we will have had time to rally our forces and defeat him."

"It could work," his mother agreed and gripped his arm. "But we must choose the opportune moment to act out our plan."

Everyone nodded and they talked over the details. His family's support filled his heart with warmth, but also with a twinge of fear. He could not get their hopes up and then fail at his task. Any small failure could mean death for them all.

CHAPTER TWENTY-ONE

A Quest

One evening, King Tristan sat in a secluded corner of the great hall while the members of the Daireann court and some of his company socialized, danced and played a few games at nearby tables. Leland even joined in on most of the dances, proving very popular among the ladies at court. Ironically, his humble cousin seemed oblivious of the extra attention. Leland's dog slept in the corner of the room, in spite of the lively music. His cousin had intended to leave Artair in Kiely, under the care of a friend, but the stubborn wolfhound had followed them all the way to Daireann, refusing to leave Leland's side.

Tristan's restlessness had abated after meeting with King Arlan, but a lonely ache in his soul took its place. The small celebration had been thrown in honor of his agreement with the king to bring Lady Airell home. Although simpler than the celebrations in his kingdom, it still served as a memory of all he had lost.

"Would you care to dance, Your Majesty?" a wispy

feminine voice asked.

Tristan looked up into a pair of hazel eyes and managed a smile at the young lady before him, in spite of his dark mood. "I apologize, Milady. I'm afraid I do not dance."

She frowned, appearing deep in thought for a moment and fiddled with the lavender ribbon weaved into the long raven braid that draped over her shoulder. "How about a game of dice then?"

He sighed in resignation and agreed, hating to refuse her second request. When she sat across from him, Tristan studied her youthful features for the first time. She appeared tall for her age, but had to be at least two years younger than him—no older than sixteen. Yet she seemed to have more maturity than most young ladies he had met in his court.

She unclasped a small pouch from her belt and took out six dice. After making the first roll, she looked back up at him. "I am Lady Gwyneth, by the way. I apologize for not introducing myself when you first arrived. I have been occupied helping care for my brother, King Arlan."

"Lady Gwyneth," he repeated, his eyes widening with recognition. "Lady Airell's sister?"

"Aye," she answered as the happiness in her eyes faded. For a moment, he recognized the same ache of loneliness in her eyes that he felt. "I wanted to thank you. My sister is very dear to me. It means so much to my family and I that you are willing to go on this quest to bring her home."

He nodded and took his turn. "I only wish I could do more...and sooner. 'Tis difficult to wait until spring to begin my journey to the north."

Gwyneth shook her head and her hand flourished

toward the people dancing. "You have done more than you realize, King Tristan. You have given my people hope. Not to mention, my brother's health has improved significantly since his talk with you. He has been feeling up to short walks...and my mother...she hasn't been out of bed in weeks, but tonight she came down to participate in the celebration."

"I did not realize." He looked down and fidgeted with one of the wooden dice. It had two dots on the top and an engraved fawn in the middle.

"'Tis amazing how one person can bring about such a change, is it not? God has sent you here with a great purpose, Milord."

Tristan looked up and stared at the beautiful young lady across from him for a moment before he had to look away again. Her eyes gleamed with such innocent faith in him. Yet she had no idea of the darkness he fought within his heart. He studied the dice again, longing to change the subject. "I hope you don't mind my asking, but what do the deer represent, Milady?"

She grinned and took one of the dice in her palm. "My sister made these for me. Airell calls me *Devin* sometimes...her *little deer*." She giggled to herself. "When I was younger, I used to skip and bound through the fields like one, or so I'm told."

A light chuckle escaped his mouth, picturing it, but Tristan cut the foreign noise short. How long had it been since he shared a laugh with someone? "I'm sure you miss her very much."

"Aye," she agreed, somber again. "We used to play games all the time...often late into the night. When she returns, I hope we will resume the tradition."

"I'm sure you will." He smiled as they continued the game, although his heart still remained troubled by the blind faith she had in him to rescue her sister from King Malcolm's clutches. He only hoped he did not disappoint her in the end.

Reagan awoke hours before the dawn to the sound of Arlan's ragged breathing. After lighting a candle she saw him shivering under his blanket. Reagan reached down and pulled the fur coverlet over her husband before pausing to feel his forehead. His skin felt hot and clammy to the touch. "Oh, my love!" she cried.

Reagan rushed to the door and opened it, telling one of the guards to fetch help. After the physician arrived, he coaxed Arlan to drink a cup of medicine to reduce his fever. She refused to leave her husband's side for hours, alternating between dabbing his forehead with a cool cloth and holding his hand.

When the dawn arrived, the physician's herbal drink seemed to work. Arlan's fever broke and he appeared to be sleeping comfortably. She stepped to the side with the physician and could tell right away from his grieved expression the news wasn't good.

"He has been doing so much better the past few days. Is there nothing else that can be done?"

The physician shook his head sadly. "We can try to keep him comfortable. My herbs will help keep the fever down, but if His Majesty's condition continues down this course, I fear the illness will eventually spread to his brain."

"Brain fever?" Her eyes widened with realization of what he told her.

"Aye, Your Majesty. I am so sorry to have to tell you this, but if that occurs, it is unlikely the king will survive."

She gulped down her emotions. "Will you please relay this news to the rest of the family and send for the royal priest? I do not wish to leave my husband's side."

He bowed. "Aye, Your Majesty. I will do as you wish."

After thanking the doctor and closing the door behind him, Reagan crossed the room and sat on the edge of the bed. "He's wrong. You're going to be fine, my love," she murmured, kissing Arlan's hand and soaking it with her tears in the process. She closed her eyes and whispered the only words she could manage. "God, we need a miracle. Please, do not take him from me."

Arlan stirred and opened his eyes. His eyebrows furrowed in her direction as he squeezed her hand. "Do not despair, my queen," he rasped. "'Tis not the end."

She smiled while smoothing some blond hair off his forehead. "Aye. You will survive this."

He shook his head and sputtered out a cough. "I meant…'tis not over for you, my love. You must go on afterwards."

Her hand moved to caress his cheek, scarcely able to breathe—heart shattered. "No, Arlan. Do not speak of leaving me. I cannot bear it. What about the future we talked about…having children and ruling side by side until the end of our days? I thought you wanted it as much as I do."

"Aye, you know I do, but it appears my life is taking a different path." He let out a deep sigh, face pinching like the words tormented him. "Reagan, when I am gone…you will no longer be the queen of Daireann. You must start planning for a new marriage alliance now…so you'll be ready when the time comes."

"No!" she sobbed and wrapped her arms around him, resting her head on his chest. "I shall never wed again."

"You will...someday." His fingers smoothed her auburn curls. "It comforts me to believe you will find love again...and I only pray this man be worthy of you."

Reagan could only cling to him. Maybe she could make him stay if she believed enough for the both of them. "Arlan...please..." Her words drifted away into the shadows of the room and silence fell over them.

A few moments later, a cough rattled in Arlan's chest. "I...I only wish I could see my sister...one last time."

"You will," she whispered, sitting up again to look into his eyes. "Arlan, you will see Airell again. We must keep faith. King Tristan has promised to rescue her."

"Aye, thank you for reminding me."

Reagan watched over him until he drifted back to sleep and then Queen Norah entered. Her eyes were red from crying—obviously hearing the news of her son's worsening condition from the physician. However, she stood straighter and with more confidence than Reagan had witnessed in several months. "My brother requests your presence on the ramparts. I will sit with Arlan while you are gone. It is of much importance."

Reagan stood to her feet in seconds. "What is it?"

"Soldiers, my daughter." She paused and a smile lit up her face as she approached and gripped Reagan's shoulders. "Our soldiers from South Rhona. They have returned."

With a prayer of thanksgiving on her lips, Reagan dashed from the room. It seemed they had gotten their miracle. Her cousin, Lord Fergus, had sent the soldiers they so desperately needed. Surely the hope of seeing Airell return to Daireann would help her husband conquer his illness.

King Tristan's heart soared when he saw the Daireann soldiers returning from Rhona. After resting a few days to recover from their long journey, a break in the cold weather spurred them all to leave on their quest early. With the king's illness growing worse, even Queen Reagan, who had been cautious of his plan at first, seemed anxious for their departure.

The morning of their quest, Tristan woke up early, donned his armor and headed out to the courtyard to prepare his new army for the long journey ahead. The gathering clouds in the distance told him the pleasant weather would not hold out long, but at least they could make a good head start before the winter reared its ugly head once again.

After going over his plans with Leland and Airell's Uncle, Lord Edmund, all the court came out to bid them farewell and wish them a safe journey. He had almost turned to mount his horse when Lady Gwyneth appeared before him. She wore her raven hair halfway up in braids with long curls cascading down the back of her silver fur cloak. A brave smile lit up her face as she placed a single die in his hand. "Praying for safety of travels for you, Milord. If you ever feel this quest is for naught, remember God sent you here for a reason, King Tristan. Through you, He has brought us so much hope already and He will help you complete this quest if you keep your faith in him." She closed his fingers around the small wooden die.

Tristan held Lady Gwyneth's hand for a moment as their eyes met again. "Thank you, Milady. Whenever I look at it, I will remember."

The raven-haired beauty didn't say another word. She simply offered an elegant curtsy and smile before disappearing back into the crowd with a swish of her lavender gown.

The young king opened his hand for a moment and smiled, seeing the image of the little deer engraved on the die. The past week, spending time talking and playing games with Lady Gwyneth could have seemed insignificant to most people, but somehow their fast-growing friendship had returned some of his humanity. He didn't realize it until now, but he had felt more like the man he used to be in her presence. He placed the die safely in the money pouch attached to his belt, willing the new peace in his heart to remain there for the duration of his quest.

CHAPTER TWENTY-TWO

Spring

Airell drew in a deep breath of air and smiled while gazing over the high walls of the watch tower. The rising sun highlighted the white and pink blooms sprouting from the tree branches and patches of green dotted the snowy cliffs. "'Tis like the land has finally awakened from her long icy slumber and donned a lovely new gown."

Tiernay approached and stood beside her, placing his hand over hers. "Aye," he answered simply and smiled, but it seemed forced, like something heavy weighed upon him.

Airell's heart quickened at the feeling of his hand touching hers. Winter had brought them closer, but neither one of them had expressed their feelings. They had been too busy planning their escape from the fortress and secretly gaining support for Tiernay.

For a moment, enamored with the change of season, she had forgotten what the change meant, but now she remembered the gravity of their situation. Airell looked up at him, eyebrow arched. "Is something wrong?"

He sighed and she knew the answer. "I apologize for waking you so early and for my silence. I simply wanted one last peaceful moment with you before…" His voice faded off in the spring breeze.

Her eyes widened in fear. "Tiernay, before what?"

"My uncle is growing restless. He received a letter today from Lord Fergus, accepting a marriage alliance with my sister. The king has decided to set sail for South Rhona tomorrow and is taking Fiona with him. 'Tis my fault. I never should have suggested an alliance with them."

Airell's hand flew to her mouth in an attempt to stifle her gasp. "Tiernay, she can't travel! Even though she has been able to hide her pregnancy with wraps and cloaks thus far, she will not be able to continue much longer. The baby could arrive while at sea."

"I know." Tiernay nodded and met her gaze. "'Tis why I convinced him to go on our spring hunting trip first. We leave within the hour." He turned to Airell and gripped her shoulders, his hazel eyes intense. "Tonight, after we have gone, I'm counting on you and my mother to lead Fiona and the rest of the court who support our cause out of the fortress safely. Slade will hide a few horses in the woods so Fiona will not have to walk. I will meet you in Dóchas Village in two days hence. Then we'll travel together into North Rhona as we planned. My cousin will take care of us there."

"Two days? Tiernay, how will you return to us? Won't King Malcolm know you've gone?"

He paused and gulped before looking at her again, eyes troubled. "Let me worry about that part of the plan. But if I do not make it in three days, you must go the rest of the journey without me."

"Go without you?" She stared at him for a moment until his words soaked in. "No!"

"You must, Airell. 'Tis the only way. Please do not be dismayed with the change in plans. When the danger has passed, you shall return to Daireann as I promised and be free of this prison."

"I am not concerned about returning to Daireann." Her voice broke and Tiernay pulled her into his embrace. Airell leaned her head against his chest, listening to his racing heart. He'd never held her so close before and she lingered in his strong arms, fearing she would break apart if he let her go.

A few moments later he pushed her back gently and bent down to look at her, but she avoided his eyes. "Then what troubles you?"

She tried to stop the words, fearing the raging emotions in her heart, but the truth gushed out of her mouth like a rushing river. "I cannot bear the thought of losing you."

Tiernay released a trembling sigh and lifted her chin until their eyes met. "Nor I you, but I must go." He caressed her cheek with his fingers and then his lips pressed against hers, leaving Airell breathless. As Tiernay laced his fingers through her golden hair, she leaned closer and kissed him in return, willing him to stay with her.

When he finally released her, she clung to his hand and drew in several ragged breaths, longing to confess what was truly in her heart while she had the chance, but she struggled to find the words. Instead, Airell wiped her tears and managed a brave smile. "Return to me safely, my husband. For whom shall I beat at chess if you do not?"

A light chuckle escaped his lips before he kissed her hand. "Aye, keep the game board ready, my wife."

Tiernay emerged through the side entrance of the fortress on horseback with his uncle, a few other nobles and a small company of guards. After crossing the drawbridge over the canal, they ventured toward a steep wooded path through the mountains. However, as the drawbridge creaked back into place behind him, he glanced back at the fortress one last time.

On top of the watchtower he caught a brief shimmer of golden hair flowing in the breeze. The sight brought warmth to his soul, knowing his lady watched him depart.

His mind transported him back to the moment they shared with each other less than an hour before—how her cobalt eyes sparkled in the morning light and the way her soft lips felt against. Tiernay's heart soared with hope. Perhaps she wished to stay with him after he reclaimed his throne. After so long, hoping she could learn to love him, in spite of his past sins, now he believed it was possible. He had been sent a wonderful gift to help him see his soul was redeemable. In recent weeks he had even made peace with his Heavenly Father and asked forgiveness for his actions in Órlaith. His soul had never felt so light and free. In spite of the danger he now faced, Tiernay knew without a doubt, God was with him.

He turned back to the trail ahead but tucked the memory of his first kiss with Airell in his heart to remind him what he had to fight for.

As the morning and afternoon wore on, they caught small game, including a few rabbits and pheasants before stumbling upon wild boar tracks and following them through the wilderness. The hunt led to no avail, but took them into a section of forest with dense undergrowth. It would aid him in his escape. By nightfall, they made camp close to a small stream and enjoyed a rabbit stew by the fire.

Tiernay retired to his tent early, but did not sleep. Instead, he stared at the light from the full moon reflecting through the fabric and listened for movement outside. When all was quiet, he gathered his pack and slipped out of his tent in silence. With the moonlight for a guide, he would travel through the night and make it halfway to Dóchas by morning's first light. By that time, Airell, his family and other supporters would be halfway there as well, only coming from another direction. If he planned it well, they would arrive by nightfall tomorrow around the same time, getting a head start before King Malcolm realized they had escaped.

Tiernay made it all the way to his horse before a twig snapped under his boot.

"Can't sleep either?"

He cringed, knowing he'd been caught and turned toward the deep voice behind him. He saw his uncle's large, menacing silhouette in the firelight.

"Aye," he answered, quickly dropping his pack out of sight and untying a small rolled bundle positioned behind his horse's saddle. "'Tis colder than I thought. I'm fetching another blanket."

As he approached, his uncle nodded and rubbed his hands over the flames. "'Tis why I stay by the fire."

By the time Tiernay reached a spot diagonal from his uncle, his heart had stopped pounding so hard. "Do you not sleep well, Uncle?"

"*Sleep*," the king scoffed. "I haven't had a decent

night's sleep in several months."

"I'm sorry to hear it."

His uncle waved away Tiernay's concern. "'Tis fine. I enjoy the night. It soothes me…and after we make an alliance with South Rhona, perhaps I will have enough gold and I will sleep more soundly."

"Aye, perhaps." The prince stared at the flames, doubting his uncle would ever be satisfied with the size of his treasure hoard. The larger it became, the more intense the king's appetite for gold grew.

King Malcolm smiled at him in the dim light, sending tingles down Tiernay's spine. "I was wrong about you, my boy. You are not at all like my brother, Donnally. 'Tis a relief I can allow you to live, unlike your father who forced my hand."

Tiernay's blood boiled, finally hearing the truth. His mother had suspected Malcolm of poisoning his father for many years—and now he knew for certain. His uncle talked so calmly about regicide and without remorse, making it clear his madness had completely consumed him. Tiernay could no longer go through with his original plan to flee with his family. His uncle would continue to murder innocent people unless someone stopped him—and there was little chance of reasoning with a mad king. Tiernay had no choice.

CHAPTER TWENTY-THREE

Moonlight

Airell paced her chambers, already donned in a traveling gown with trousers underneath, boots and a warm hooded cloak. Her satchel was packed with an extra pair of clothes, food, her journal of stories and her favorite book of poetry from Tiernay's study. Now she only had to wait for the signal to leave.

As she continued to pace, her eyes fell to the chessboard on the small table by the window. Airell stopped and held the ebony king in her palm, studying the tiny details Tiernay had carved himself. She smiled, remembering her last moment with him at the watchtower. She had promised to keep the chessboard ready, but now she realized it was all for naught. It was too big to fit in her satchel, but at least the pieces could be saved. Without a second thought, she stuffed all of them into her satchel, hoping it would give her peace, having something of Tiernay's with her until they were reunited in Dóchas.

A few moments later, commotion filtered through

her door from the hallway. She heard a group of guards rushing past and then a faint knock. Airell peeked out the door, smelling a hint of smoke in the air.

The guard, Peadar, stood at her door. "The time has come, Your Majesty. You must go now." Then in an instant, he was gone.

Rushing back into her room, she found the candlestick and set fire to the bedspread and tapestries. After the blaze started to grow, Airell threw the strap of her satchel over her shoulder and slipped into the hallway, leaving the door wide open. The way was still clear of guards, but beginning to fill with smoke. She covered her mouth and nose with the hem of her cloak and navigated the dimly lit hallway. After a few turns, she heard more guards and hid in the shadows while they passed. Then she continued before colliding with someone coming from the other direction.

"Isla!" she rasped in a low voice and hugged the girl close for a moment.

"I'm sorry, Milady. I waited under the staircase like you asked, but I got worried and returned to find you."

"'Tis, all right. Come, we must make haste."

They reached the narrow stairs to the lower levels of the fortress as more commotion erupted from above. Then they hurried down the steps, into the darkness below and hid beneath the staircase, holding each other close.

Torches lit up the darkness as about a dozen guards rushed past. She heard more coming and knew they would have to take the alternate route. It would take longer, but they couldn't risk going any further. They felt along the wall under the staircase until something gave way—a hidden door, only large enough to crawl through.

Airell went through the opening first and then waited for Isla to squeeze through before closing the door behind them. They crawled through cobwebs and Airell let out a faint gasp when her hand touched the furry back of a large rodent she couldn't see in the darkness.

It squealed and skittered past, toward Isla. She screamed and Airell clamped her hand over the girl's mouth until it was gone. They sat in the darkness for a moment, listening. Then Airell took her hand away before whispering to Isla in a calm voice. "We have to remain calm. If someone hears us, it will put everyone in danger. Think of something else—something pleasant and calming."

"Aye, Milady," she answered and they continued on.

For several minutes they crawled along, encountering a few more rats, but Isla didn't cry out again. When they approached large cobwebs, Airell did her best to clear them away to make it easier for Isla. The whole way, Airell whispered scripture from Psalms 23, helping them both to keep their sanity.

"Yea, though I walk through the valley of the shadow of death, I will fear no evil: for thou art with me; thy rod and thy staff they comfort me..."

After what seemed like an eternity of darkness, Airell felt something solid ahead and gave it a firm push. The hidden door gave way and Airell saw torches, highlighting the top of a low narrow cave. It was taller than the passage they had just crawled through—about six feet, she guessed and several dozen adults and children came out of the shadows. The men had to stand hunched over to avoid scraping their heads on the jagged stone ceiling. They had all come from different secret passageways to avoid drawing attention. Thankfully the fires had kept Malcolm's men occupied while they all escaped.

In spite of the troubling circumstances that brought them down into the cave, Airell couldn't hide the proud smile on her face. These were the brave nobles and servants of Brannagh—the ones who had pledged their loyalty to Tiernay—their true king.

"Oh, my dear one," Queen Ciara whispered, weaving through the crowd with Lady Fiona trailing close behind. The queen mother enveloped her in a tight hug. "I worried you were captured."

Airell breathed a sigh of relief. "We had to hide from some guards and took the backup tunnel, but we made it." She looked around at the familiar faces of her ladies and maids. "Is everyone here? Slade? Peadar? Did they make it out, too?"

The large bulky guard came out of the shadows with two other guards loyal to Tiernay on both sides. All three bowed before her. "At your service, Your Majesty."

She nodded in approval and smiled, but it faded as her eyes darted around frantically looking for the servant boy's face. "Slade? Where is he?"

She turned to Isla, whose eyes were filled with tears. "I haven't seen him since supper."

Airell let out a strangled gasp and started to move back toward the secret passage. "We have to find him!"

"No!" The queen grabbed her arm, pulling her back. "Airell, we must go. Slade will find his way out and meet us in Dóchas. 'Twas his village and he knows the way."

Airell stifled a sob and shook her head. "I cannot abandon him."

The queen kept a firm grip on Airell's shoulders,

eyes intense in the dim cave. "From what I hear, Slade is brave and clever. He will find us. I believe it with all my heart." The queen swept her hand toward the citizens of Brannagh. "These are now your people and they need you to lead them to safety. Tiernay will be waiting for us. We have to make haste or we will be putting his life in danger as well."

Airell looked at the glowing faces around her, realizing the truth of Queen Ciara's words. As much as she loved Slade like a younger brother, it was her duty as the future Queen of Brannagh to protect her people and the rightful king as well.

She wiped her tears and nodded slowly. "Aye, we must go."

Airell followed Queen Ciara and Lady Fiona down a winding passageway, holding a torch for light. It seemed like an entire lifetime passed by when they reached the end. Then the queen unlocked a hidden door and pushed it open.

The fresh air rushing in through the opening and the bright full moon above them sent relief rushing through her body. After spending the winter months trapped within the confines of the fortress, the thought of being free exhilarated her.

However, they'd only made it a few feet from the exit when alarm replaced her relief. Voices echoed in the cave behind them.

"Come, we must make haste," the queen urged. "The guards are not far behind us."

Airell stood frozen for a moment until Peadar appeared with the two other guards. All three knelt on the cold ground with Peadar in the center. He kissed her hand. "You needn't worry, Your Highness. We will hold them back as long as we are able."

"No!" Tears streamed down her cheeks. She couldn't let them sacrifice their lives for her.

"It has been a pleasure to serve you, Your Majesty." A smile spread across his broad face. "Now my wife and daughter await my arrival. I will be reunited with them soon."

Before Airell had a chance to protest, Peadar stood and drew his sword. The other two followed suit and rushed after their leader, back into the darkness of the cave with loud and valiant battle cries.

Queen Ciara grabbed Airell's arm, pulling her along, toward the safety of the woods. "Come, let us not make their sacrifice be in vain!"

Airell used the moon for a guide as she fled Malcolm's guards through the woods with the rest of the Brannaghn citizens. Queen Ciara led the way with Fiona by her side, while several men stayed at the back, making sure all the women and children were accounted for. Some carried children on their backs if they couldn't keep up with the group.

They hadn't been able to find the horses without Slade's help, but started making good headway regardless. Things were going well and they could no longer hear the men pursuing them when Fiona cried out in pain and crumpled to the ground. "I cannot run anymore. I…I think the baby is coming!"

The group came to an abrupt halt as Queen Ciara and Airell knelt by her side. "We must keep moving. There is a midwife in Dóchas," the queen urged and they both helped Fiona stand and then worked as a team to support her as they continued on through the night at a slower pace.

When voices and footsteps behind them grew closer, Airell knew their decline in pace had cost them. Soon Malcolm's forces would catch up.

"Separate," the queen urged the people behind them. "Separate into smaller groups and hide in the brush. 'Tis our only chance."

Airell's heart pounded as she hid with Queen Ciara, Fiona and Isla. Everyone else ran in separate directions with small family groups and hid as well.

Footsteps approached and she held her breath. Fiona curled into a ball in the grass, shivering violently. Helpless, Airell put her hand on her sister-in-law's shoulder, trying to provide comfort. She knew very little about childbirth, but feared for Fiona and her baby. All the stress and physical exertion they'd endured couldn't be healthy for them. If only the plan to leave on Tiernay's ship had worked, or if they'd had enough time to find horses Slade hid for them, but there was little time to think of what could have been. Now it was her duty to keep everyone safe.

A light rain pattered on the forest floor, filling the air with an earthy aroma as the footsteps became so close they almost seemed to be right on top of them—then silence.

Airell waited a moment before exhaling in relief. "I think they've passed," she whispered.

Isla slowly lifted her body to peek out from behind the bushes when a large hand grabbed her arm. She let out a piercing scream.

"What do we have 'er?" a man's harsh voice cackled. "I knew we hadn't lost them. They be hidin' in the brush!"

Isla wriggled in the man's arms and bit down on one of his fingers to make him release her.

Airell leapt out of her hiding place without a second thought and tackled the man. He was caught off guard and they rolled in the wet grass. Airell's shoulder scraped on a tree root, snagging the fabric.

"Isla run!" She cried out while scrambling to her feet, but to her dismay, several soldiers wearing hoods appeared and they were surrounded.

Airell backed up, only to be caught by the man she had tackled earlier. "You are a feisty one," he growled, the hot air from his mouth blowing on her neck.

She stomped on his foot which made him loosen his grip for a moment, but then he seized her arm and wrenched it behind her back. Airell cried out as something popped in her wrist.

One of the hooded men in front of her lifted a bow and arrow, but to her surprise he did not aim it at her, but at the head of the mountain of a man behind her. "If you wish to live, release the lady at once."

CHAPTER TWENTY-FOUR

The Hunted

Within a few seconds after the hooded men appeared, more filled in behind them—soldiers. She recognized the style of their armor and knew in an instant they were from Daireann. As the large man behind her loosened his grip on her arm, Airell heard yelling and the clashing of swords in the distance. She knew it had to be more unseen soldiers fighting off Malcolm's men who'd pursued them into the woods.

The first hooded man stepped closer, rain dripping off his dark cloak. "I said, *release* her."

With a sudden movement, the man behind her obeyed and then tried to dash off into the overgrowth. He didn't get far before a few soldiers caught up with him.

The archer lowered his bow and studied her in the dim light. "Are you injured?"

She shook her head, but then winced, holding her throbbing wrist. Her shoulder stung as well, but she brushed it away for the time being. "'Tis only a scratch.

Who are you, Milord?"

The rain stopped and the man lowered his hood. "King Tristan of Órlaith."

"Tristan!" Isla shouted and rushed into the king's arms. "Oh, Cousin. 'Tis so good to see you alive! How did you get here?"

Tristan looked just as shocked as Airell felt. "I should ask you the same, Cousin. We thought you had perished in Órlaith."

Finally, Isla turned and motioned toward her. "This is Princess Airell of Daireann. She saved my life and helped me pose as a servant in Brannagh."

Airell froze and then managed to curtsy, her heart thumping wildly, after seeing Tristan for the first time since childhood. It seemed like ages since she had accepted his proposal. Much had changed since then. He had become king and she had wed another. Yet, she couldn't stop studying his face in the dawn's faint light. Even with his golden hair and beard shaggy and his face smeared with grime from travelling, he was still strikingly handsome.

The king hesitated for a fraction of a moment in surprise before stepping forward and kissing her hand. "Thank you for looking after my cousin. Please accept my apologies for not recognizing you, Princess."

"'Tis understandable." She looked down at her disheveled traveling dress, torn and caked with dried mud and leaves. "I must be quite a sight." Airell shook her head, not even wanting to imagine how her hair looked with spider webs, leaves and dirt tangled into it.

The king didn't seem to notice and smiled for the first time. "You are a lovely sight to behold—even more so after journeying such a long distance to find you."

Airell's eyes widened. "You came all this way for me?"

"Aye, your brother gave my quest his blessing."

Tears stung her eyes. "Arlan lives?"

"Aye and he speaks of nothing else than reuniting with you," Tristan answered, but his smile faded. "He sent your uncle, Lord Edmund, to bring you home safely in his stead. He waits in Dóchas with the rest of our army, helping set up camp."

Tristan's change in mood concerned her. However, she had little time to ask questions.

"Isla!" someone shouted and a handsome young man with dark, shoulder-length hair pushed his way through the crowd of soldiers, accompanied by a large black and gray dog.

"Leland!" Isla shouted and launched herself toward him.

He caught her in his arms, the momentum nearly toppling them both. "My dear sister," he replied, squeezing her even tighter as happy tears rolled down his cheeks. "I thought you and Mother to be dead. Oh, praise the Lord it was not true. Is she with you?"

Isla frowned and whispered the truth in his ear. Then, Airell's heart twisted, watching them quietly weep in each other's arms.

Fiona's faint groaning from behind the bushes brought her back to reality and she rushed to her sister-in-law's side as Ciara held her close. Her skin had taken on a pasty white tone and she shivered violently in the morning breeze.

"What ails the lady?" Prince Tristan asked.

Airell gripped the young woman's hand. "Princess Fiona is with child. I fear she and the baby may be in danger. We were headed to Dóchas. There is a midwife there."

"Aye, we departed from the village last night. 'Tis only a few hours from here and they will be able to help her." He turned to Leland who nodded after a silent exchange between them. "My cousin will travel ahead of us with Lady Fiona." At Airell's reluctant glance, he continued, his intense green eyes convincing her to trust him. "He is the best horseman in my company. Believe me, I trust him like a brother and he will bring her there safely—and in half the time it would take on foot. A few soldiers will accompany them."

Airell nodded, although still worried about Fiona's reaction to riding on a horse with a stranger, but deep down knowing it was her best chance at survival.

Leland left for a moment and returned with his horse. King Tristan lifted Fiona with care and then helped her get situated in front of his cousin on the saddle, tucking a blanket around her. She shuddered at first as he wrapped his free arm around her, but then relaxed her head against his shoulder, seeming too weak to protest.

Leland looked down at Queen Ciara and Airell with calm, reassuring brown eyes. "I will do everything in my power to bring her to Dóchas safely. You have my word."

The sincere expression in Leland's eyes made Airell believe every word of his vow even though she did not know him. However, the queen still appeared uneasy. Without a second thought, Airell turned to Queen Ciara and squeezed her hand. "You should go with them. Fiona will need you." She started to protest until Airell gave her a determined look, speaking volumes about her loyalty. "I will stay behind with them and see you in a few hours. Like you said, they are now my people as well."

After a teary hug and whispered thank you, the queen climbed on the back of a soldier's horse to leave with Leland and Fiona, however Isla opted to stay behind with Airell, refusing to leave her side. Leland protested at first, not willing to part from his sister so soon, but Isla won the argument, insisting she would see him in a few hours.

After the men and women on horseback left, King Tristan gave her a wary glance she couldn't quite decipher, but Airell couldn't worry over trifles at the moment. It was her duty to ensure the people from the fortress arrived safely in Dóchas.

King Malcolm and his hunting party awakened before dawn and after a hasty breakfast, Tiernay had no choice but to leave with them. They followed the boar tracks and halfway through the day, when his group finally discovered the herd, Tiernay used the opportunity to slip away. He hid behind the undergrowth until the company passed by and then journeyed parallel to them, listening in to see if they noticed his absence. As thirty minutes passed, they were so engrossed by hunting the boars, they didn't notice anything had gone awry.

Guilt almost caused Tiernay to abandon his plan, until seeing a squealing boar run almost directly in front of his path, pursued by his uncle. He crouched behind some dense brush as his uncle stopped and raised his bow to make the kill. It was in that moment, only feet away from the man who poisoned his father, Tiernay saw his chance. With Malcolm's back turned to him, concentrating on the boar, Tiernay stood from his hiding place and stringed an arrow on his bow, aimed at his uncle's back. If it was a clean and precise hit, he might not even suffer or know what hit him.

Tiernay's hand trembled for a moment, the gravity of the situation hitting him full force. Could he take his uncle's life? *God if there is any other way, please show me now*, he prayed. When no answer came, he thought of his family and Airell and knew he had to protect them.

Sweat dripped down Tiernay's brow as he re-aimed the weapon to compensate for his uncle's slight movement. His fingers poised to release, when an awful roaring squeal sounded behind him, followed by fiery pain in the back of his calf. Tiernay stumbled back in shock and the arrow flew on its own. He fell to the ground in agony as the boar rushed past him and disappeared into the undergrowth.

After coming to his senses, Tiernay tore a piece of fabric from his shirt sleeve and wrapped it around the gash in his leg. Then he heard a man groan and scream from the other side of the brush and he peeked through the branches to see.

Commotion ensued as others rushed to help the wounded king. His uncle had been hit in the thigh instead of the back. Now he only had one choice—flee before anyone found him.

King Tristan stayed silent while bandaging and splinting Airell's left wrist. It wasn't until they stopped for a break when she finally admitted to being in pain. He had dreamed of meeting her again for so long and seeing her now took his breath away. He tucked in the final piece of bandage to make the wrapping hold and then he looked into her sky blue eyes. "A physician needs to take a look at your wrist once we arrive in Dóchas to make sure it is not broken, but the splint should keep it from moving until then."

She gave him a shy nod. "Thank you, Milord. Not only for bandaging my wrist, but for intervening last night."

"If only I could have found you sooner. I could have prevented you from getting injured." He hung his head, remembering his thirst for revenge. He had to put it aside now and make sure Airell made it back to Daireann with her uncle, like he promised. Then and only then, could he focus on conquering the Dark Lord and his nephew.

Airell sighed. "Let us not speak of what could have happened. I am thankful you were there when you were."

"Aye and now you will return home with your uncle, where it is safe. Then, after we defeat the Dark Lord and Prince, we can put this entire nightmare behind us once and for all. I will return to Daireann and we can have a proper betrothal, like I always intended us to have." Lady Airell broke his gaze and stared at the dirt beneath her feet, confirming his fear. "Milady, are you having second thoughts?"

She shook her head with a sad expression. "I am afraid I do not understand my own thoughts. I am married to Prince Tiernay. 'Twas not something I wanted to happen, but it did—and now…"

"You were tricked into a fake marriage alliance," he interrupted. "Your brother told me."

"Aye, but Prince Tiernay had every intention of letting me return after our escape…but I no longer wish to leave here. As strange as it seems, among the people of Brannagh, I feel at home."

Tristan exhaled in frustration. "You wish to stay?" She nodded miserably and he continued. "Milady, I understand you have made…friendships here, but there is no need to be a martyr. You have helped the innocents of Brannagh escape the clutches of a mad king. You have even selflessly cared for the family of our greatest enemy. 'Tis enough. The time has come to leave this place. Soon the King and Prince of Brannagh will no longer be alive to hold you captive."

"Like I said before, Prince Tiernay is not the one who was holding me captive. I have fallen in love with him," Airell blurted out and Tristan stopped breathing for a moment at the shock of her words. They were like arrows straight through his heart. Had he journeyed all this way only to be rejected, in favor of an evil prince who did not even deserve to live, nonetheless win the love of someone as beautiful and pure as Lady Airell? "I never wanted to marry him," she continued, "but I thought you had perished in the attack on Órlaith and I had to do what was right for my people. I apologize, Milord, if I have hurt you. I never intended for any of this to happen, but I cannot betray my own heart."

"You do not know what you are saying," Tristan replied, pausing to catch his breath. "The Dark Prince is one of our greatest enemies. He took part in the sieges against both our kingdoms. How could you love such a monster?"

"He is not the man you think he is. King Malcolm blackmailed him into doing those things. He had no choice."

Tristan gritted his teeth. "Everyone has a choice to do good or evil. You have been in captivity for months, Milady. I do not blame you for being confused. These people have a way of manipulating the innocent."

"I am not confused," she huffed. "The king threatened to kill his family. He was just as much of a prisoner as I was."

Tristan puffed air in frustration and then walked away from her to untie his horse. However, in spite of his own feelings, he turned around once more. "I made a vow to your brother to return you safely to Daireann. Will you not even return for his sake?"

"My brother will understand. I must follow my heart."

Tristan let out a deep sigh and his voice softened. "Your brother is dying, Milady. He wishes to see you one more time. After you return to your homeland, it is up to you to decide what you will do or where you will go, but at least honor a dying man's final wish."

Tears dripped down her cheeks and Tristan died a little on the inside, wishing to comfort the princess in her grief. However, it was beyond his ability at the moment. Lady Airell had made it clear she didn't long for him to comfort her. She loved another—someone who did not deserve her.

CHAPTER TWENTY-FIVE

Reunited

Airell stayed up late after arriving in Dóchas, helping to calm Lady Fiona during her labor. Finally, about an hour before sunrise, her sister-in-law gave birth to a beautiful baby girl with a full head of chestnut brown hair, just like her mother.

Fiona held the little bundle in her arms—still pale and weak from the previous night's events—but smiling so radiantly it lit up the entire tent. "Clare," she whispered. "Her name will be Clare, for God has sent a bright light into my life, even during these dark days."

After admiring Baby Clare for a few minutes, Airell returned the infant to Fiona and stepped outside the tent to get some fresh air. There, she found Leland nervously pacing with his wolfhound in tow. She didn't know Lady Isla's elder brother well, but sensed he needed encouragement. "Lady Fiona had a healthy baby girl," she told him, grasping one of his arms so he would cease pacing.

He breathed a relieved sigh and his kind brown eyes

gleamed with happiness in the dim light. "Thank you. I am pleased to hear it. And Lady Fiona? How is she faring?"

"Very well," she reassured. "And we have you to thank for getting her to the village in time. Now, try to rest, Milord. I believe a long day awaits us."

"Aye, Your Majesty." He headed off toward his tent, appearing light on his feet and full of cheer. His genuine concern for Lady Fiona—a young woman he barely knew—was quite an endearing quality. She loved Leland's gentle spirit right away. In some ways he reminded Airell of her brother.

A bright smile lingered on her mouth while strolling along the outskirts of the village as the early light of dawn filtered through the tree line, but then her grief from yesterday returned.

She still couldn't grasp what Tristan told her about Arlan. Could her brother really be dying? It seemed impossible to imagine life without him. Lady Reagan had to be completely devastated, as well as her mother and sister. Now she knew she had no choice but to return to Daireann—at least for a while. Her family needed her there and she needed them.

Then she remembered Tiernay. Right now, if everything had gone as planned, he was close to Dóchas, but had no idea he walked right toward more danger. Would Tristan kill him on site if he found him? It was a terrifying thought. How could she leave him at a time like this?

Airell was so distraught, she didn't even notice someone trailing behind her in the shadows, until the man pulled her into his arms behind some high bushes and gently clamped his hand over her mouth.

"Airell, don't scream," a familiar voice whispered

and the hand dropped from her mouth. "'Tis only me."

After the fear passed, Airell focused on the man's face in the dim light. "Tiernay." With sudden realization she wrapped her arms around his neck and pulled him to eye level. For a moment, all her worries drifted away in his presence. "I love you," she whispered in between chaste kisses and then paused to let out a faint chuckle before looking into his hazel eyes. "I do not know why it took me so long to admit it."

Tiernay smiled and kissed her one more time before holding her against him and smoothing her golden hair with his fingers. "And I love you, Airell...with all my heart."

Tiernay held Airell in his arms for a long time with his eyes closed. After being away from her for two days, not knowing when or if he would see her again, it felt heavenly to simply hold her. Seeing the unfamiliar soldiers camped out in Dóchas had alerted him to approach with caution, but her kisses almost made him forget about the possible danger.

After a few moments she leaned back and touched his cheek. "I was so worried."

"You needn't worry any more. I'm here now." He reached down to take her hand in his, but paused, noticing the bandage. His brow furrowed in concern as he gently lifted her injured wrist to inspect it. "What happened?"

Airell closed her eyes for a moment and released a shuddering breath. "We were captured by your uncle's men. One of them twisted my arm behind my back. It doesn't hurt too much now."

He kissed her fingers, relief flooding through him.

"I am glad to hear it. And what of my family?"

She managed a weary smile. "They are fine. You're an uncle now, Tiernay. Fiona delivered a healthy baby girl only an hour ago. She named her Clare."

Tiernay's heart soared. "Praise be to God. He protected all of you. I will have to see them soon. But I must know, how did you escape Malcolm's men?"

Her smile widened. "My brother sent soldiers from Daireann. They intervened when we thought all hope was lost."

"I'm glad they arrived in time, although I am sure they would not be pleased to see me here. I will have to take extra precautions to not be recognized until they realize I am no longer an enemy."

Airell shook her head and gripped his shoulder. "Tiernay, there is something you should know. Something I've been keeping from you. King Tristan led the army here."

His eyes narrowed in disbelief. "*King* Tristan? He's alive…and here in Dóchas?"

"Aye, he saved us…but he wants to kill you, Tiernay. 'Tis not safe for you here." She took his hand and pulled him further into the cover of the woods. "You must leave now, before someone sees you."

He grimaced and limped behind her. Airell took notice of his discomfort and looked down at the cloth cinched around his calf and encrusted with blood.

"Oh, you're hurt!"

He nodded and drew in a sharp breath. "A wild boar slashed me with its tusk. 'Tis painful, but it will heal with time."

"Here, let me look." She helped him sit at the base of a large tree and knelt beside him. Tiernay rested his back against the tree trunk while she inspected the wound. For the first time, he realized how weak he felt. He had lost quite a bit of blood on his journey to Dóchas.

Airell frowned and squeezed his hand. "Most of the bleeding has stopped, but it needs to be cleaned and stitched closed. Just try to rest and I'll return soon with supplies." He nodded and closed his eyes until she returned with a bucket of water, supplies and a piece of bread. She cleaned his wound, stitched it and then wrapped his calf with a clean bandage. "There, it should heal fine now."

He thanked her and after eating the bread, and drinking some water, Tiernay felt better, but remorse nearly blew him over. "I—I tried to kill my uncle, Airell. I shot him with an arrow, believing it was the only way to keep everyone safe."

Her eyes filled with tears. "You did?"

"Aye, but I failed. The arrow did not kill him. 'Twas all for naught. I fear I only made everything worse."

She cupped his cheek in her palm. "You returned to me. 'Tis enough for now."

He shook his head and placed his hand over hers. "You do not understand. He knows I have betrayed him and he will never stop until all of us are dead. I need to destroy the ships like we planned. It will weaken him."

"But how? You will need more men."

He paused, rolling the thought over in his mind and calculating the risks. "King Tristan and I have a mutual enemy. With help from him and the army from Daireann..."

"No!" she interrupted, eyes filled with terror. "If Tristan discovers your presence here, he will not hesitate to kill you."

He sighed and gazed into her eyes. "'Tis a risk I must take to save the ones I love. Somehow we have to get everyone to safety in North Rhona. You should travel north with my mother and sister. When this is all over, I will meet you there."

Airell hung her head and he knew in an instant something had changed. "I don't know if I can go with your family anymore." When she looked up, her chin quivered and her eyes filled with tears. "My brother's health is failing and he longs for my return home. But how can I leave you at a time like this? I do not think my heart can survive being torn in two different directions."

He pulled her sobbing form into his arms and they sat under the tree for a while with her head resting against his chest. She sniffled quietly, soaking his shirt with her tears and then quieted. Tiernay had never felt so lost—knowing the right thing to do in his heart, yet in his mind wanting to be selfish and keep the treasure he held in his arms forever. He had only reunited with her an hour ago and now they would have to part again. If he let her go back home, would she ever return to him?

In the end, Tiernay rested his cheek against her golden hair and forced himself to whisper the heart-wrenching words he dreaded. "Go home, my love. Your family needs you."

She looked up at him and shook her head with tears rolling down her cheeks. "But *I* need *you*."

He cupped her cheek in his palm, wiping her tears with his thumb. "We shall be reunited again someday, if your heart still desires it."

"Of course it will. My heart has chosen you. That will never change," she whispered before kissing him and snuggling her head closer to his neck. However, as Tiernay held her a little tighter before she had to return to the village, he couldn't shake the fear his plan would fail and this would be their last embrace.

CHAPTER TWENTY-SIX

Betrayed

In the afternoon, King Tristan stood in the shadow of his tent, watching a hooded figure creep past the walls of the village. The woman held a small cloth-covered food basket in one hand and a pail of water in the other. She looked like a peasant at first glance, but the longer he watched, he could tell from the elegance of her walk, his first assumption had been wrong.

Tristan left in silent pursuit after her as she journeyed parallel to the wall at first and then disappeared behind some tall bushes. He paused for a moment and then trailed her path. After emerging through the bushes she was nowhere in sight, but he heard a slight rustle in the undergrowth ahead and followed the sound. He had almost reached it when a rustle from behind stopped him.

Tristan's hand flew to the pummel of his sword, but barely had it drawn before the tip of a blade flicked against the back of his neck.

"Drop your weapon," a man's voice ordered. "I do

not wish to harm you—only to talk."

He gritted his teeth. "Your sword digging into my neck would suggest otherwise."

Airell emerged from the bushes with a grieved expression on her face. "Please listen, Milord," she pleaded, her blue eyes filling with tears.

Tristan obeyed and tossed it aside. He seethed under his breath, knowing he had walked right into a trap. Airell had betrayed him.

The other man relinquished his blade a fraction of an inch away from his skin. "Turn slowly."

When Tristan did, his eyes narrowed, staring into the face of his enemy with contempt. "Prince Tiernay. Have you returned to finish what you started months ago?" He lifted his arms outward—chest heaving in and out. "Go ahead. I have nothing left to lose."

Tiernay lowered his sword, revealing his weakness. He was a few years older, a bit taller and had more experience with the sword. However, under pressure, he hesitated—he showed empathy. "I told you before, I only wish to talk…and beg for your forgiveness. What I did to you in Órlaith was inexcusable, but the time has come to put aside this rift between us. We have a mutual enemy and if we work together, Ardena will be at peace once again."

Tristan raised one eyebrow in suspicion. "You would turn on your own kin? I find that hard to believe."

Tiernay clenched his jaw and a storm brewed in his hazel eyes. "King Malcolm is no longer my kin. He poisoned my father, stole my birthright and threatened everyone I love. He needs to be stopped before he kills again."

Tristan nodded. "'Tis one matter we agree on."

The prince let out a sigh of relief and moved to sheath his sword.

Tristan saw his chance. He lunged forward, knocking the other man off his feet and for a moment they rolled on the ground, grappling for Tiernay's sword which had landed a few feet away.

Airell screamed for them to stop in the background, but in the heat of the moment he didn't care. The young king only heard his own murderous thoughts and thirsted for sweet revenge.

He landed atop his enemy and pummeled his face repeatedly in a blind rage. Traumatic images flashed through his mind. His father slain on the battlefield—his kingdom reduced to ashes and smoke—the prince's blade slicing across his chest before he plummeted into the sea.

As Tiernay groaned in pain and choked on his own blood, Tristan dug his knee into his ribs to keep him immobilized while slipping a dagger from his boot. He sneered in victory while pulling the blade up to his enemy's throat. "This ends now. My family and kingdom will finally be avenged."

"No!" Airell screamed. "Don't do this, Tristan. If you ever cared for me at all, I implore you. Please allow him to live."

On the ground, the prince let out a choked breath and looked past Tristan to Airell, his eyes full of sorrow. "Please, look away, my love. Remember I..."

Tristan twisted the blade against his neck, barely enough to draw blood. "Do not *speak!*" he growled through clenched teeth, digging his knee deeper into his ribs, causing Tiernay to cry out in agony. "You do not deserve the luxury of final words." Tristan lifted the dagger above his head, ready to plunge it into his enemy's chest.

"Wait!" Tiernay coughed and looked him in the eye. "K-kill me...if you m-must. I...deserve it. Just promise to protect her...from Malcolm...please."

The desperate look in the other man's eyes caught Tristan off guard and he froze. Moments from death, his enemy did not beg for mercy—in fact he admitted he deserved to die. His only concern was for Princess Airell and her safety. Did he have some good in him after all?

"Please Tristan," Airell sobbed and collapsed next to them on the ground. "Show mercy!"

Tristan's hand trembled as he held the dagger, poised over Prince Tiernay's heart, struggling to make a decision. Finally he let out a guttural, animal-like roar and stabbed the blade into the ground beside his enemy's head, leaving it sheathed there for the time being, along with the murderous rage in his heart. Killing Tiernay wouldn't bring his family or kingdom back. It would only haunt him for the rest of his life.

Moments later, soldiers arrived, drawn by Airell's screams. Tristan's strength dissolved away and he slid onto the grass next to the prince, breathing hard. "Take this man to the village. Tend to his wounds and keep him under guard."

Tristan sat behind his tent, shivering by a small fire. An untouched pail of water sat nearby, but he stared at his bloody knuckles in a fog. How had he come to this point? How had he come so close to murdering someone? His soul had never felt more lost—more broken.

A hand rested on his shoulder and Tristan looked up into his cousin's calming brown eyes. Leland didn't say a word, but draped a blanket around Tristan's shoulders and sat beside him in silence for a while instead. His cousin had been sleeping during the whole ordeal after staying up all night, but he had no doubt heard what happened by now.

Tristan sighed and pulled the blanket closer around him with one hand and patted Artair who rested in the dirt by his feet. The dog's warmth brought him comfort. "How is the climate of the village with the Northern Prince's arrival?"

Leland shrugged and poked at the dying fire with a stick. "Mixed. Most of the soldiers from Daireann want him severely punished or even executed for taking their princess, of course, but the nobles from the fortress and the villagers want him released. They see him as their king."

Tristan nodded. "Well, I already gave him a severe beating. Perhaps that will satisfy the Daireann people at least." He frowned while contemplating what to do next, waiting for his cousin to impart some kind of wisdom as he usually did.

After several minutes, Leland broke the silence, but did not mention the incidence in the woods. Instead, he fed another log into the fire and gazed at the flames licking around it. "Back in Órlaith, when the battle was over, I had never felt more hopeless, seeing the kingdom reduced to ash. I felt like a failure."

He turned to his cousin while warming his hands over the fire. "You were braver than any of us. You saved so many people and brought them safely to Kiely, myself included."

A sad smile spread across Leland's face. "Aye, Cousin, but I was knocked unconscious at the beginning of the battle."

"You were?"

He nodded. "An enemy shield struck me in the head. When I woke up by the edge of the harbor, I only saw death and destruction all around me at first. I thought everyone I loved had perished. Then King Malcolm approached, reveling in his victory. He was so close I could have touched his boot. I remained still, pretending to be one of the dead. When he passed I grabbed a sword. With his guards nearby, I knew taking my revenge would be my last act on this earth, but reasoned the sacrifice would have been worth it."

Tristan stared at his cousin in amazement. "You could have killed him? What stopped you?"

"I heard God's voice, like a whisper directly to my heart. He said, 'vengeance is mine.'" Leland paused to compose himself and when he looked back at Tristan, tears clouded his eyes. "Shortly after King Malcolm passed by, I saw a glint of chainmail floating in the water out of the corner of my eye. It was you, Tristan, clinging to the rocks below the cliff. You were barely alive—half drown—but seeing you there brought me hope. I knew God had stopped me from killing Malcolm so I could save you. He still had a future in mind for our people—a future with you as king." Leland patted Tristan's shoulder. "I know you may not see it now, but God still has a purpose for your life, Cousin. You'll understand more clearly in time."

Tristan stared at the fire, thinking over Leland's words long after his cousin left. He washed the blood from his hands and face. Then he reached into the money pouch attached to his belt, taking out the gift Lady Gwyneth had given him before leaving Daireann. Studying the deer engraved on the wooden die, he smiled, remembering her words had been similar to Leland's. God still had a purpose for him. Tristan grasped the die in his hand, willing himself to get up off the ground. He didn't know if it was true, but he had to finish his quest regardless.

CHAPTER TWENTY-SEVEN

Allies

Every bone and muscle in Tiernay's body ached as he sat on the hard dirt floor of a small hut, hands and feet bound with rope. His face and ribs pained him the most, but he would live. He couldn't blame King Tristan for almost killing him. The plan to talk to him had been risky, but in truth, even though Tiernay was in a great deal of pain, a huge weight had been lifted off his shoulders. He wasn't a murderer after all. Tristan survived his fall and Tiernay had asked his forgiveness. It was a start at least.

The thatched door swung open and Airell entered with a pail of water, bandages and food. He attempted to smile, but feared it looked more like a grimace.

Her eyebrows furrowed with concern while sitting next to him. "How are you faring?"

"Much better now that you are here. I thought King Tristan ordered one of his men to come and tend to my wounds."

Airell managed a faint smile. "I insisted on being

the one. You are my husband after all and the soldier had dirty hands. I didn't trust him." He chuckled at her disgusted expression, causing him to grimace and cough. "I'm sorry. Here, let me look at your ribs." She lifted his shirt and drew in a sharp breath while observing the angry purple bruising already beginning to show up on his abdomen. He winced as she applied gentle pressure to his ribs. "Well, it looks awful at first glance, but nothing seems to be broken. Is the pain terrible?"

He nodded and grimaced again. "It comes and goes in waves, but I'll survive."

She lowered his shirt and dipped a cloth into the water. Then she carefully washed the blood and dirt from his face, taking care around the various cuts and painful bruising around his left eye.

"Do my mother and sister know what happened yet?"

She shook her head. "They are sleeping after the long ordeal the night before. I have kept it secret thus far."

He nodded as relief washed over him. "Good, there is no need to worry them."

When she finished cleaning his wounds, he managed a lopsided smile. "I assume this is not what you expected a marriage would be like. Constantly having to tend to my wounds?"

She shook her head. "Not at all." He let out a deep sigh of regret and looked down before she lifted his chin. Her loving gaze warmed his heart. "'Tis even better, my husband. I never expected to find such joy, or love so deeply."

His heart pounded in response. "Nor I. In spite of all the hardships we have been through, your love is a gift from God I would never trade."

Airell smiled and gave him a gentle kiss on his forehead—the one part of his face that didn't hurt. "I feel the same."

The door swung open slowly as King Tristan and his cousin, Leland, came into the hut. The king turned in Airell's direction and gave a slight bow. "We would like to speak with the prisoner alone for a few moments if you wouldn't mind, Milady."

She stood, gave King Tristan a wary glance and placed her hands on her hips. "I do not intend to allow you to hurt him again."

"I will not lay a hand on him. You have my word, Lady Airell."

Leland nodded in agreement. "I will make sure of it, Your Majesty. You needn't worry. Things will be kept civil while I am present."

Airell seemed to trust Leland's promise more than his cousin's, but still looked uneasy.

"I'll be fine," Tiernay insisted and his reassurance seemed to satisfy her. She touched his shoulder briefly before leaving. Then he found himself alone with the king and his cousin. "So, what did you wish to speak to me about?"

Tristan paused for a long moment before asking Leland to cut Tiernay's restraints. "I have reconsidered your proposal to work together. Although I still have some reservations, you are the only one who knows the secret passages inside the fortress and can predict what your uncle might be planning. In truth, I have no other choice. The success of this quest depends on your help."

Tiernay smiled and then grimaced, rubbing his sore wrists. "So, we shall be allies?"

A slow grin crept across the king's face as he took

his hand and helped him stand. "Aye, Prince Tiernay, if that is what you wish to call it. Allies we will be."

CHAPTER TWENTY-EIGHT

Departing

The next morning, Airell gazed at Tiernay as the sunrise emerged on the horizon, highlighting the little village with a golden glow. His face looked worse than the day before with his left eyelid swollen all the way shut, but she didn't care. He was still handsome in her eyes. "Stay safe, my love."

He smiled before kissing her hand. "I will. We still have a chess game to finish, don't we? Do you still have the game pieces?"

She nodded. "Aye. I'll keep them safe."

Her uncle approached with his horse. "Airell, you have to bid him farewell now. We must make haste."

She nodded and kissed Tiernay one last time, lingering in his embrace, but careful not to hurt his bruised ribs. "Farewell is such a painful word," she whispered, trembling against him, emotions already raw from saying goodbye to his mother, sister and niece in the tent.

He leaned back to look into her eyes, his chin quivering for a moment before regaining his composure. "Then neither of us will say the word. I'll see you soon.

Is that better?"

She smiled and nodded as he wiped away her tears. "Aye, see you soon."

Airell's uncle helped her onto the horse and they waited for a moment as Isla bid a tearful farewell to her brother and cousin. Then Leland helped her onto the back of Airell's horse. She made eye contact with Tristan's kind-hearted cousin whose face pinched with worry over his sister's well-being. "I'll watch over her like she's my own kin. You have my word. We'll see you in Daireann soon."

Leland nodded as Isla sniffled behind Airell. "Thank you, Your Majesty. I am in your debt."

She squeezed his hand for a moment and then looked over at Tristan who nodded with a faint smile on his lips in response. His silent exchange spoke a thousand words to her soul, conveying he had forgiven her for what had transpired between them the past few days. Hurting him was the last thing she wanted and guilt had tormented her, wondering what could have been. However, now she hoped they could at least be allies in the future—and maybe even friends.

Moving away from Dóchas, Airell turned one more time to look at Tiernay, praying she would see him again. Gazing at him in the golden light, she remembered all they had been through in such a short time. They had shared a lifetime of adventures. The experience had challenged and changed her—yet she realized she wouldn't have it any other way. Their hearts had grown together gradually and unexpectedly—so much it hurt to part with him. No matter what happened in the coming days or what people in Daireann would say about him, Tiernay was her choice.

After watching Airell depart, Tiernay shared a few final moments with his mother and sister as they prepared to leave for North Rhona with the rest of the survivors from the fortress.

His mother embraced him one last time. Then tears filled her eyes as she stepped back to study his bruised, swollen face. "I fear for your safety, my son. How can I leave you with these people after their leader nearly killed you?"

"I will be fine, Mother. God will be with me and I have supporters from the fortress and Dóchas who will protect me." He managed a lopsided smile and held her hand. "This is something I must do for the future of our kingdom and the safety of our family. Please go with Fiona. It will ease my soul knowing you are both safe in Cousin Ewan's kingdom. I will send for you when it is safe."

After his mother nodded and let Tiernay go, he hugged Fiona, careful not to crush tiny baby Clare who she held in a sling close to her body. "I'll see you both soon."

"Aye," his sister agreed, trying to sound brave, but her body trembled in the cool spring air and tears dripped down her pale cheeks as she turned to go.

When his family approached their awaiting horses, Tiernay studied the small group of survivors from the fortress waiting to leave, observing their ragged appearance. There were mostly women and children in the group, as most of the able-bodied men had decided to stay behind with Tiernay for the battle.

"They do not have enough protection, Milord," Leland said to King Tristan as they came up from behind, voicing Tiernay's unspoken concerns.

The king folded his arms over his chest. "What do you propose we do, Cousin?"

Tiernay watched in curiosity as Leland glanced in Fiona's direction for a moment and then back at Tristan. "We should send some of our soldiers to accompany them."

"Aye," Tristan agreed with a thoughtful look in his eyes. "You should accompany them as well."

Leland's eyes widened in surprise. "How could I abandon you during the most crucial time in our quest?"

Tristan forced a smile. "You are not abandoning me, Cousin. This is an important mission. When you arrive in North Rhona, I will need an ambassador to negotiate an alliance with King Ewan. He has not been receptive in the past, but now with our war against King Malcolm, perhaps he will reconsider. We will need all the support we can get."

Leland still looked reluctant, but bowed before his king in submission. "As you wish, Your Majesty. I will join you back in Kiely soon."

A few moments later, Leland bowed before Tiernay as well, vowing to protect his family and people during their journey north. Then he watched as the king's cousin approached Fiona. He gently grasped her hand and held it for a moment. His sister—usually terrified of men—visibly relaxed in his presence, filling him with relief. She needed a protector in his absence. After a brief exchange, Leland helped Fiona climb onto the front of his horse, taking special care to ensure her infant daughter was safe, too. Then, after wrapping a blanket around her, he climbed up behind and reached around Fiona to grasp the reins.

Tiernay watched them leave with his mother and the rest of the survivors. Then he glanced at Tristan, whose indistinguishable expression sent a tingle down his spine. Did the king have an ulterior motive for sending Leland away?

Regardless of his suspicions, Tiernay sent up a silent prayer for the safety of his family and Airell who travelled back to Daireann with her uncle. No matter what happened in the next few days, at least they would be safe.

It took a day and a half's ride to reach the harbor. Then the rest of King Tristan's company set up camp in the woods while he scouted out the area with Prince Tiernay.

"Not good," the prince whispered as they hid in the undergrowth. He pointed toward Solas Castle by the sea. "Malcolm has moved from the fortress. He's here. Those are some of his personal guards standing by the gate."

Tristan gripped the pummel of his sword, gritting his teeth. "Good, he's closer than we thought. It will be easier to find him and kill him."

Tiernay shook his head and grimaced, clutching his sore ribs for a moment. "No, not easier. 'Tis going to be much harder. If they were at the Dub Hach fortress, there would have only been enough soldiers to guard the ships. But now we are greatly outnumbered. Also, look at the ships. They're loaded down and ready for departure. Some of them have already left early, but we can still destroy the ones remaining."

Tristan blinked hard and clenched his jaw. "Well, we must act tonight then. We do not have a choice."

"Aye," Tiernay agreed. "It will be more dangerous than anticipated, but we have to try. We cannot risk the chance of Malcolm making it back to Daireann and putting Princess Airell and her kingdom in danger again. None of these ships can leave the harbor."

Tristan listened to the prince's plan, even though deep down he wished to bypass the whole detail of burning the ships. He wanted to find King Malcolm alone and kill him, using any means necessary. The past few months, Leland had acted as his voice of reason, which was why he couldn't allow him come along for this part of the quest. Tristan would not let anyone talk him out of what he had to do next.

CHAPTER TWENTY-NINE

Sacrifices

Tiernay stared at the sunset in the evening before the attack on the harbor as a foreboding feeling passed through him. He didn't fully trust King Tristan, yet *he* controlled most of the army. Tiernay had to work with him and play his part in the plan. His bruised ribs throbbed from the long journey to the harbor as well, but he tried to ignore the pain and concentrate on the task at hand.

As night fell, Tiernay and Tristan prepared the best twelve archers in their company. Then they left the rest of the men under the command of Ciaran, the highest ranking Darieann soldier and set out into the darkness, taking the long way through the woods to avoid being seen. They scaled down a craggy cliff by the sea one by one and then along a narrow ledge until reaching a small inlet near a cave where four spare rowboats awaited them. Tiernay paused to catch his breath, holding his sore ribs for a moment. Then he nodded in approval and ordered the men to gather dry driftwood to make a fire in the cave, out of sight from Malcolm's men and wait for the signal. Every part of the plan had to be carried out at the right time in order to work. If they started toward the ships too soon, attention would be drawn and the army would overtake them before they had a chance to set them ablaze.

Tiernay stayed near the edge of the cave for what seemed like an eternity, waiting for the signal. Finally, he heard it—war drums and horns echoing from the ridge above. The Daireann commander had spread out their forces, like they had planned, making their army seem larger than it was. As he watched, men scrambled from their night guard positions and rushed to protect the castle. They only left a few by the harbor to protect the ships. He grinned with the realization everything had gone as planned so far.

After making sure most of the soldiers near the harbor were gone, Tiernay motioned for three of his twelve men to subdue the ones remaining. Then almost simultaneously, the remaining soldiers split into three groups, torches in hand. They only lit one per boat and kept them low to avoid too much light. Then, after a signal from the three men on shore, they rowed into the harbor, setting off in different directions.

Tiernay and Tristan headed out in the last boat and navigated toward the two largest vessels—King Malcolm's and his own. They rowed hard, knowing it would take them longer than everyone else because the larger ships had to be anchored out in the deeper water.

They paused rowing for a moment, hearing a battle cry from the ridge in the distance. They saw the two armies clashing together, with theirs having the high ground. It was exactly the distraction they needed.

At the signal, the men in the boats released flaming

arrows at the boats, lighting up the night sky. Fire reflected in Tiernay's eyes, as he focused on reaching the last ships.

Pulling up beside his ship, Tiernay paused for a moment, not wanting to destroy it. The vessel had come to represent freedom for him, but he couldn't risk letting it fall into enemy hands. Gritting his teeth, he lit an arrow with the torch, strung it on his bow the same time as Tristan and they both released. Within a minute or two, the deck exploded into flames.

Then they aimed flaming arrows at his uncle's ship. However, to his horror, the deck came alive with activity, awakened by the commotion from shore. Men were moving around the deck, trying to douse the flames.

"Malcolm is on board. I know it," Tristan hissed while loosing a few more flaming arrows. "He's been there the entire time—taunting me. Look at that." He pointed toward the men on the deck, busy trying to raise the sails. "They are preparing to set sail. I must find a way to board the ship and stop him."

Tiernay shook his head and smothered the torch in the water so they wouldn't be seen. "No, he's my uncle. 'Tis my duty to end this once and for all. If we can get close enough without being seen, I can throw a grappling hook up to the side of the hull and climb up with a rope. It could work."

Tristan paused for a moment and stared at him, appearing to think over his plan. Finally he nodded in agreement. "You prepare the hook and I'll steer you as close as I can."

Tiernay attempted to calm his nerves as they approached his uncle's ship. He knew his plan had a slim chance of success and it would most likely be his last act on earth. Yet, what other choice did he have?

When they came up beside the ship, Tiernay swung the rope with the grappling hook and launched it upward, pleased when it anchored onto the edge of the hull at his first attempt. He took a deep breath, praying for courage and then turned toward Tristan. "For what it's worth, I'm glad to have called you my ally in the end."

A slow grin spread across Tristan's face. "And an unlikely friend."

"Aye," Tiernay agreed with a nod and turned to grab the rope before pausing again, eyes fixed on the starry night sky as a wave of sadness washed over him. "If I do not survive this night, please tell Princess Airell my last thoughts were of her. Will you watch over her for me?"

He heard Tristan shift one of the oars behind him, most likely trying to steady the boat in the waves. "You will see her again, my friend...sooner than you think."

Tiernay started to turn, thoughts tangling in confusion, but was met with a wooden oar to the head. The force of the blow sent him backwards, landing like a rock in the bottom of the boat. A burst of colors filled his vision and then all faded into darkness.

"I'm sorry, my friend," Tristan whispered. He clung to the rope while pushing off on the rowboat with his boot. "This is my fight. I couldn't let anyone stop me."

He watched the rowboat with Tiernay's unconscious form inside it, drift further into the harbor, toward shore. Then he climbed up the rope attached by the grappling hook Tiernay had thrown. Tristan had almost made it to the top before the ship began to move. He climbed over the edge without being noticed.

Half the crew members were too busy trying to douse the flames and the other half of the men were raising the sails.

Tiernay's men in the rowboats had approached the ship and were launching more fiery arrows at the deck and sails, unaware he was onboard.

Then Tristan saw him—King Malcolm barking out orders. He had a limp from where his nephew shot him with an arrow, but still appeared fierce and dangerous with a hint of madness glowing in his dark eyes.

Tristan saw his opportunity to stop the Dark Lord once and for all. He approached slowly, hood pulled over his head and eyes fixed on his target. When he got close enough, he drew his sword and the reflection of flames danced across the metal.

At the same time, one of the king's guards noticed Tristan and surged toward him, blade drawn. Heart thumping, he deflected the other man's advances, ducked under his arm and then coming up from behind, bashed him in the back of the head with the handle of his sword. The guard fell to the deck unconscious.

When another guard charged his direction, Tristan fought him off as well, sending the man careening head first off the side of the ship.

In his determination to get to the king, Tristan felt invincible. He charged forward to challenge three more guards. Then he heard King Malcolm's low voice barking orders from nearby. When the guards stopped in their tracks, Tristan locked eyes with the king.

Malcolm sneered in his direction and then turned back to his guards for a moment. "Return to your duties. Save the ship. This one is mine."

Tristan stepped forward as the atmosphere disintegrated around them. One of the sails had caught fire now and some of the men had abandoned ship by diving overboard. However, his focus stayed completely on the evil king before him.

Malcolm drew his sword and his sneer of reproach widened. "I've seen your face before. Aren't you King Donovan's weakling son? I should have taken care of you myself instead of leaving the chore to my treasonous nephew. I won't make the same mistake a second time."

Tristan surged forward with a battle cry and their swords clashed together twice before he pushed the king's blade down and struggled to keep it there for a few moments. Their faces close together, Tristan clenched his teeth and growled. "The time has come for you to pay for the evil things you have done."

The king cackled, his eyes wild. "Many have tried and failed to kill me. You will be no different." He forced his sword upward and out of Tristan's control. Even with an injured leg, the Dark Lord was much larger and stronger than Tristan and he knew it. However, the young king was determined to defeat him or die trying. For what seemed like an eternity, Tristan advanced, battling Malcolm with every ounce of strength he had within him.

Then with a swift move, his opponent's sword sliced across his upper right arm. Tristan cried out in pain and his sword dropped from his grasp.

King Malcolm lunged forward, pinning Tristan to the side of the ship, his blade aimed at his throat. He could feel the man's hot breath assaulting his face. "Any last words?"

Tristan took in shallow gasps of breath to prevent the razor sharp blade from slicing into his skin. After a few moments he grinned, knowing a secret the king did not. "Long…live…King Tiernay." Surprise registered across Malcolm's face and Tristan took the opportunity to grab the dagger from his belt and plunge it into the king's abdomen. He doubled over with a grunt, dropping his blade from Tristan's neck.

Instantaneously an arrow arched over the deck, hitting the captain in the chest. The man grasped the arrow and slumped over the wheel, jerking it all the way to starboard. The boat soon followed sharply in the same direction, throwing everyone off their feet and rolling across the deck.

Tristan forced himself to his feet as the mast, now engulfed in flames, cracked in half and slammed across the length of the ship. As everything fell apart before his eyes, he peered over the hull of the ship for a moment, seeing the outline of large rock formations jutting out from the shore. They would hit within a matter of seconds unless someone turned the ship.

Tristan jumped into action, dodging flames and debris rolling across the deck. He had almost reached the captain's wheel when a hand clamped around his ankle, sending him plummeting to the deck face first. He turned over, groaning as the metallic taste of his own blood filled his mouth.

"You cannot kill me that easily," the evil usurper rasped while standing above him.

Tristan stared past him toward the stars twinkling above, remembering Lady Gwyneth's words about God having a great purpose for him. Had he ruined everything by betraying Prince Tiernay in exchange for a chance at revenge? Was there any hope left for his redemption?

I'm sorry. He prayed. *I let the thirst for revenge consume me. Forgive me, God.*

When Tristan focused on Malcolm again, the Dark Lord cackled with a sword poised over his chest.

Tristan clamped his eyes shut, believing it to be the end—but the blade never reached him. Instead, a violent jolt shook the entire ship along with a deafening crack as the prow slammed into the rocks. An explosion of debris clouded the air and the ship tipped savagely to one side. The sea vessel moaned, snapped and gurgled as it took on water.

Tristan rolled across the deck and clung to the crippled hull. Flaming debris fell from above, singing his skin and gurgled screams from the crew members flooded his eardrums. His muscles twitched from exertion and an agonizing groan escaped his lips as he struggled to hold on. Then with no strength left at all, Tristan's fingers lost grip. His body slammed into the frigid water below, plummeting down, deeper and deeper until fiery red dissolved into black.

CHAPTER THIRTY

Daybreak

Tiernay faded in and out of consciousness as the row boat rocked in the gentle waves from the harbor. He gazed up at the stars for a moment, wondering why Tristan would betray him. Then his head throbbed again, blurring his thoughts and forcing him back into a lethargic sleep.

The next time he awakened, his face and lips stung—baked from sun exposure. The boat had stopped drifting and he heard water lapping against land, making the boat tilt toward the shore, each time a wave hit it. He opened his eyelids and then squeezed them closed in shock of the bright sun above him.

After a few minutes, he tried again, turning his head to avoid the direct sunlight the second time and allowing his eyes to adjust. Then, Tiernay forced himself up and rolled onto the shore with a groan of agony. He dragged his aching body up the rocky beach and struggled into a sitting position.

Tiernay rested for a moment to catch his breath and

then looked around, deciding from the location of the rock formations his boat had come to rest near the edge of the harbor, past the cave. If he had drifted any farther, his boat may have gone out to sea. He whispered a prayer of thanksgiving before his eyes drifted to the horizon and the smell of charred wood drifted toward him. Smoke curled from the wreckage of a ship smashed against the rocks and sinking in the waves—King Malcolm's ship.

Tiernay struggled to his feet and limped toward the sandy part of the beach, heart twisting at the sight before him. "Tristan!" he screamed, half out of anger and the other half, grief. There was no reply and he screamed again, seeing wreckage and bodies washing up on the shore. "No!"

His throat burned and his mouth felt dry and salty, but Tiernay continued to scream and rasp until collapsing into a trembling heap on the sand. Tristan had betrayed him, but he had also sacrificed his life to complete their quest. His actions had saved Tiernay's life.

He stayed curled up in a ball on the sand among the wreckage for a long time, not hearing anything except the sound of the waves lapping against the shore. When the sun began to set, a hand touched his arm. "Your Majesty, are you hurt?"

Tiernay rotated his head slowly and recognized a familiar face above him, covered with dirt and grime. "Slade?"

The boy smiled and Tiernay had never been more relieved to see his servant. Slade helped him sit up. "Aye, Your Majesty. Come, the rest of the survivors await us in the castle."

Four days passed while Tiernay recovered from his wounds at the castle. After years of neglect, the old structure was covered with a thick layer of dust and cobwebs, but his servants managed to clean and refurnish the king's chambers for Tiernay to stay in them comfortably. Although, each morning he woke up in his parents old chambers, he didn't feel like the ruler of his kingdom. He didn't feel like a king at all. His mother, sister and the rest of the survivors from the fortress had yet to return, even after he sent his fastest riders to find and accompany them home before they reached North Rhona. Without them there, the castle felt desolate and lonely.

Tiernay wandered to the terrace outside his new chambers and gazed toward the harbor where the army had worked to clean up the debris and recover bodies from the water. A few hours before, they identified the body of his uncle, but it didn't bring him satisfaction. Instead it only summoned additional grief and pain. The price of victory had cost them dearly—his people had lost too much—suffered too long. Would the staining blood of war ever wash away from the shores of his homeland?

"Your Majesty?" Slade called to him from behind. "Your family has returned, along with the rest of our people."

Tiernay turned and clapped Slade on the shoulder, smiling for the first time in several days at the servant boy who had now become more like a younger brother. "Thank you."

A few minutes later, he rushed through the great hall—which had been converted into an infirmary for wounded soldiers—as fast as his throbbing ribs would allow him. Then he burst into the courtyard as his mother and sister dismounted their horses, joined by the surviving citizens from the fortress. He rushed into their open arms, weeping tears of joy. "It's over," he choked out. "It's done. Malcolm is dead."

"I know, my son," his mother replied in a soothing tone while wiping the tears from his eyes. Her knowing look told him she shared the grief throbbing in his heart. She understood everything and cupped his cheek in her palm. "Now I can finally say, long live the *true* King of Brannagh."

Tiernay nodded and lingered in his family's embrace, pausing to smile at his sister and kiss his niece's downy head. All of a sudden, the desolate castle seemed a little warmer with their arrival. He let out a deep sigh of relief and motioned toward the castle entrance. "Come, let us go inside."

They nodded, but Leland approached, eyes full of concern. "I have heard my cousin hasn't been seen since the battle. Has he been found?"

Tiernay gulped down a lump in his throat as he put his hand on Leland shoulder, trying to prepare him for the news. "I'm sorry. King Tristan fought bravely and sacrificed his own life to defeat King Malcolm. His body has not yet been recovered from the sea, but my men will continue searching until he is found. The King of Órlaith will forever be remembered as a hero in our land. He gave my people back their freedom."

Leland's chest heaved and his face contorted with grief. The dog sitting at his feet whined, troubled by his owner's grief. After a few moments, Leland recovered and wiped a tear from his cheek. "His body has yet to be found. There is still hope."

"Aye," Tiernay agreed, his voice thick with emotion. "Hope is something we must always hold on to."

Leland nodded, gave a slight bow and walked past him, toward the harbor with his dog trailing close behind. The determined set of his shoulders told Tiernay the Earl of Kiely didn't intend on giving up on his cousin any time soon. In witnessing Leland's determination to find his king, God showed Tiernay a tiny glimpse of the future—hope of the people of Ardena coming together—not by force like his uncle desired—but to create peace and a new, prosperous future for their beautiful land. They would never give up hope—even when things seemed bleak.

Trembling and overcome with emotion, Tiernay walked back to the comforting arms of his family and they entered the disheveled castle. The despair began to lift from his heart, knowing the little seed of hope God had planted there would grow from the ashes with time. It symbolized a new beginning for them all.

CHAPTER THIRTY-ONE

Homecoming

Airell's heart soared and then broke moments later as her homeland came into view. The journey had been long and exhausting, taking over three weeks by horse-back. Every muscle in her body ached mere seconds ago, but now she scarcely felt it. She only thought of reuniting with her brother, Arlan and the rest of her family. She prayed for a miracle—hoping maybe King Tristan had been misinformed and her brother would rush out of the castle to welcome her home. Yet, when she entered the courtyard with Isla by her side, the mood was quiet and somber. Her sister and a few members of court were the only ones who came out to greet them.

"You're home," Gwyneth whispered, pulling Airell into a tight embrace.

"Aye, it all seems like a dream."

They wept in each other's arms for a moment until she finally pulled back. "Oh, *Devin*," Airell exclaimed while studying her little sister. "You have grown even taller and lovelier in my absence...no longer a child, but a beautiful young lady!"

Gwyn gave her sister a radiant smile. "I am pleased you noticed."

Airell nodded and then turned serious, remembering the reason for her return. "How is our brother?" The troubled look in Gwyn's eyes sent fear rippling through her. "Am I too late?"

Gwyn shook her head, "No, Arlan still clings to life. I believe he waits for you."

"We must not delay then." She linked her arm through her sister's for strength and they headed inside the castle and down the long corridors leading to the royal chambers.

Gwyn and Isla waited outside and when Airell entered, time seemed to slow. The room was deathly silent as she approached Arlan's bed, surrounded by her family members, the priest and the physician who prepared a cup of medicine for the king.

Her mother was the first to notice her presence. She approached and her eyes filled with tears before pulling Airell into a tight embrace. "Welcome home, my daughter. I have prayed so long to see this day. If only it was not tainted with such grief." She glanced in Arlan's direction for a moment and then back at her. "I will take my leave so you can have your time with him." Airell gripped her mother's hand one more time before she walked out of the room and motioned for the others in the room to follow.

Then only her sister-in-law remained by Arlan's side. Reagan looked pale and thinner than Airell remembered, but stronger than ever somehow. She gave her a sad smile, before leaning over the bed to kiss Arlan's forehead. "Wake up, my love. Your sister is here to see you."

Arlan's eyelids fluttered open and he looked around expectantly. "Airell?"

"Aye, she has returned home."

Reagan motioned for Airell to sit in her place by the king and then gripped her shoulder lightly for support before leaving the room.

Airell sat on the edge of the bed and held her brother's hand, shocked at how frail he had become in her absence. He had lost weight—his cheeks gaunt and skin pasty white—yet, his tear-filled eyes glimmered with hope. "Oh, my brave sister. You have returned."

She managed a shaky smile. "Aye, because of you. King Tristan and our soldiers rescued us from King Malcolm's men after we fled from the fortress."

A few ragged coughs tumbled out of his mouth. "And what of the prince? How did you escape him?"

"I did not have to escape from Prince Tiernay. 'Twas my choice to return and he urged me to go after hearing of your illness."

Arlan's blue eyes widened at her words. "Perhaps the Prince of Brannagh has some good in him after all."

She nodded as a tear dripped down her cheek, concerned about her husband's well-being, but she quickly wiped it away. "Aye, Prince Tiernay has been kind to me. He is not who he seemed to be at all. It turns out he was a prisoner to King Malcolm as well, but now he has found the courage to fight for his rightful place on the throne."

"And it appears…you have grown to love him as well?"

Airell blushed, realizing she couldn't hide anything from her elder brother. He always seemed to know her innermost thoughts. "Aye," she whispered. "I love him very much."

He managed a frail smile and squeezed her hand, his breathing becoming more labored. "I am glad...to hear it. My prayers...have been answered. You are safe and happy...in your new life. Now I can leave this world...in peace."

"No, Arlan!" she pleaded and leaned over to hug him, sobbing against his shoulder. "You're going to live, brother. I only just returned. You cannot leave me now!"

A deep rattle sounded in his chest before speaking again. "Do not despair, sister. We both know...this is not the end. Farewells here in this world...are only temporary. We will meet again."

Airell sat up and squeezed her brother's hand again, smiling through her tears. "Aye, we will. Someday I will meet you *and* father again...but not yet. There is so much more to say."

His eyes brightened. "Perhaps I still have some strength left in me after all, Sister. Tell me more...about this prince who has proven himself worthy enough...to earn your love."

For a few days after Airell's return, Reagan was encouraged to see Arlan's health improve. Some color even returned to his face and he felt well enough to sit up in bed.

He ordered a celebration be thrown in honor of his sister's return. Although he was too weak to attend, he still enjoyed sampling some of the food and talking with his family who had gathered around his bedside after the event. Reagan had gazed at Arlan's smiling face and then the happy faces of his family with joy in her heart.

Was it the beginning of the miracle she'd been praying for?

Before falling asleep that night, Arlan kissed her lips gently and held her close. "I am a blessed man," he whispered, "to have been given a love such as yours, my beautiful Rhona bride. The years we have shared together have been a gift from God."

"There will be many more to come, my love. Many more," she whispered before falling asleep and dreaming of their future—a life full of happiness, children and growing old together.

The next morning, Arlan did not awaken with the dawn like usual. His congestion was typically the worst in the morning, causing him to cough and wheeze, but now he was still and peaceful. Reagan wrapped her arm around him and snuggled against his shoulder, treasuring a few moments alone with her beloved husband.

She recalled how opposed she had been to falling in love with him at first. Yet, he never gave up trying to win her heart during the first year of their arranged marriage. Arlan brought her freshly cut wildflowers every morning for a week straight after she came down with a severe illness. When her fever spiked, he scarcely left her side. After Reagan recovered, her heart softened toward him. They formed a friendship and eventually it turned into something more.

Now, taking his hand in hers and kissing it, Reagan loved him so deeply, she couldn't imagine living in a world without him.

When one of the servants knocked on the chamber door, Reagan was forced to rise and accept the truth. Arlan wasn't breathing. He had slipped away moments before the dawn. Her sweet and gentle husband had left her.

She called for the servant to wait outside and did her best to make the king look presentable—crossing his arms over his chest and straightening the blankets around him. Then she padded across the room in a dull haze and mustering all the poise she could manage, Reagan opened the door.

The servant bowed with a tray in hand. "Your breakfast, Your Majesty."

Reagan barely heard the girl—staring blankly at the stone wall behind her instead. When she responded, her words came out flat and detached from the true emotions trapped deep within her heart. "Please send for the royal family and the priest at once. The king is dead."

King Tiernay knelt before the cross within the walls of the castle as tears of gladness flowed down his face. The chapel had been boarded shut by his uncle when he banned Christianity from being practiced. However, as one of Tiernay's first acts as King of Brannagh, he ordered the boards be removed. Now he took in everything in awe of God's deliverance. After years of neglect, the House of the Lord had been covered with a thick layer of dust and cobwebs, but now all had been restored.

He bowed even lower in reverence, humbled and trembling as the presence of God overwhelmed him. He had restored everything—given his people back their home—their freedom—their lives.

"Thank you, Lord…for your mercy and forgiveness," he prayed, voice trembling. "I am your humble servant. Help me to become a king who brings honor to your name."

When he had finished praying and all was silent again, Tiernay felt a hand resting on his shoulder. He looked up into his mother's caring, hazel eyes. "He heard you, my son."

They embraced and then walked down the hall together, stepping out on one of the terraces overlooking the sea. Tiernay smiled, watching the seals sunning themselves on the beach and the gulls rushing around on stick legs, searching for tiny fish in the surf. "I never dreamed I would be standing here like this again. I never dreamed I would be king."

His mother squeezed his hand. "I have prayed every day for this moment—when Brannagh would be ruled by her true ruler—a king who would seek God's path above his own. Now I am blessed enough to see it come to pass with my own eyes."

"Thank you, Mother. I only pray I can become worthy of this responsibility." Tiernay gazed out at the sea and breathed in the salty air. Over a month had passed since the attack on the harbor. The soldiers from Daireann and citizens from surrounding villages had helped clear away the debris and now were helping rebuild homes and ships. It would take time, but soon the Solas Castle would be restored to her former glory.

His uncle had been given a proper burial in spite of the evil he had done. However, King Tristan's body had never been found. The mystery gave Tiernay hope. Perhaps his friend had survived the shipwreck somehow. However, as time passed, the notion soon faded from his thoughts. His cousin, Leland, refused to give up though and traveled up and down the coast, searching with a small company of men.

Fiona had become quite dependent on Leland and temporarily retreated back into her shell when he departed. However, her infant daughter, Clare kept her busy and in the weeks following, she seemed content to simply walk along the beach with her young daughter and enjoy the sun they had been deprived of for so long.

Memories from the past year troubled Tiernay's sleep often and he worried about Airell. She hadn't written. However, he remained thankful to God for his deliverance and held onto faith that with time they would all find healing from past wounds.

"Your Majesty?" a voice said from behind.

"Aye?" Tiernay turned toward his servant, Slade and smiled.

The boy smiled back at him and bowed "You have received a letter from Daireann, Your Majesty."

Tiernay thanked Slade and opened the letter after he left, heart pounding. After scanning the words on the parchment, he frowned and read through it again, slower than the first time.

His mother's eyes filled with concern. "Was it from Princess Airell? Is something wrong?"

He refolded the letter and let out a deep sigh. "King Arlan is dead. She must stay in Daireann for now."

The queen mother covered her mouth. "Oh, that is the reason she did not write. She must be devastated! Tiernay, you must go to her."

He furrowed his brow and looked away from his mother. "This changes everything. Airell is the Queen of Daireann now and shall never return to Brannagh. She has her own kingdom to look after and will not leave it to be ruled by a regent." His face contorted with grief, knowing what he had to do. "I will honor our alliance, but release her from the heavy burden our marriage has caused. If we have an annulment, she could find a suitable match with a nobleman in Daireann. 'Tis the least I can do for her."

"How do you know she wants the annulment if you never have the courage to ask? Let it be her choice." Her voice softened as she touched his cheek and gently turned his face toward hers. "You both deserve happiness, but you must fight for it."

He managed a sad smile and took his mother's hand. "I must think more on this. There is much to consider."

After she retired to her room, Tiernay fixed his gaze on the horizon, imagining Airell standing somewhere in her own kingdom thinking of him as well. It seemed like an eternity since they had parted ways in Dóchas, but he could still imagine her beautiful face, cobalt eyes and golden hair clearly in his mind. With all his heart he longed to see her again, yet the fear of rejection consumed him. Now she was back home—back where she belonged and had more responsibilities resting on her shoulders than ever before. Would she still choose him?

CHAPTER THIRTY-TWO

Mourning

The next month was a great time of sorrow for Airell's family and the kingdom of Daireann after they laid their beloved king to rest. He was buried beside his father, grandfather and all the other great kings of their land who had gone on before.

Airell did her best to carry on, even in her grief, taking her rightful place as queen. The people would look to her now for leadership and she did not intend to let them down.

After Arlan's funeral, Reagan requested a lesser room even though Airell protested at first—and once she had it—the young widow withdrew inside her chambers and did not come out for several weeks. Airell came by to check on her sister-in-law often, but was always turned away until one morning toward the end of spring, she invited her in.

She found Reagan sitting at her desk penning a letter. She still wore a black mourning gown like Airell did and her auburn hair—usually hanging in unruly ringlets down her back—was now carefully braided and gathered into a bun at the back of her head.

"Thank you for seeing me, Reagan. I lack anything of importance to say, but I miss you. I think of you as my sister and I do hope we can be close again."

Reagan paused for a moment and looked up, her green eyes attentive, but still dull and empty. "I miss you as well, Airell. Would you care to take a walk with me in the gardens?"

She agreed and a few minutes later they were strolling past her father's favorite rose bushes. The gardener smiled at them and snipped off two white roses from a bush, presenting both to them.

Airell thanked the elderly man and inhaled the sweet aroma from the flower while gazing over the wall overlooking Beatha Valley.

Reagan stood beside her and let out a deep sigh. "I remember first coming to Daireann. It seems so long ago. I was only a child—so young and wild—full of dreams." She let out a slight chuckle and then snipped it off quickly, like the gardener had done with the rose stems. "I was determined to be a burden to your family at first. I thought my bad behavior would make your parents send me back to Rhona."

Airell nodded with an amused smile. "I remember well. Wasn't there an incident where you pushed Arlan into the mud?"

"Aye, the first time he tried to hold my hand." Reagan grinned, but then turned serious again. "I had my heart set on marrying another and was bound and determined not to love Arlan. I decided our marriage would be an alliance and nothing else, but he slowly worked his way into my heart. And now he's gone." She rotated the rose in her hand, gazing at the white petals in silence for a while. When she did speak again, her voice sounded thin and monotone. "I think part of me died with him. The tears will not come. Why can I not weep for my husband, even when I long to, Airell? People around the Daireann court must think me heartless."

"'Tis not true." Airell placed her flower on the wall and hugged her sister-in-law tight. "We all grieve in different ways, but God has a way of healing hearts and emotions. It will get better in time. You'll see."

Reagan stepped back and smiled at her. "Thank you, Airell. I have missed our talks."

"I'm available whenever you need me."

Her sister-in-law's face turned serious. "I'm afraid it may become harder soon. I am returning home in the summer."

Airell's breath hitched somewhere within her chest. "So soon?"

"Aye." She turned and gazed out over the valley again, her voice so thin it nearly carried away on the breeze. "My mother has requested my return. We have been writing to each other in coded letters. She fears Lord Fergus is getting too comfortable on my throne. He has been making decisions without my consent. I know that now because of his hasty failed attempt at a marriage alliance with Brannagh. There have also been rumors of unrest in the kingdom. My mother is urging me to make a new marriage alliance." She paused and turned toward Airell. "I do not know if I'll ever be ready to wed another. 'Tis unfathomable at the moment."

"So what will you do?"

Reagan shrugged. "I'm not certain of the details yet, but one thing is becoming clearer to me now. I have been away from home for too long. Now I am no longer Queen of Daireann and therefore have nothing keeping me here. It is time to remind the people of South Rhona who their queen is." She paused and for the first time, Airell noticed a twinge of fear in her sister-in-law's eyes. "If only I could remind myself as well."

She gripped Reagan's shoulders, trying to infuse some additional strength into her thin frame to help her endure the difficult task ahead. "Remember, my sister, God has made you brave and strong—a queen who will lead her people in faith and prosperity. And as long as I am queen in this kingdom, you will have Daireann as an ally." She paused and smiled through her tears. "Will you promise to write often?"

Reagan embraced her again. "Aye, my sister. As often as I am able.

As spring retreated and summer arrived, Lady Reagan's departure for South Rhona left a void in Airell's heart. It almost felt like losing Arlan all over again, yet she tried to carry on the best she could manage. Her duties as queen kept her busy most of the day, but at night she watched the flames in the hearth and thought of Tiernay.

He had responded to Airell's letter, telling her of King Tristan's presumed death. The news saddened Airell greatly, but her sister took it the hardest. It seemed she had formed a friendship with the king when he spent time in Daireann. However, she took Isla under her wing and they seemed to comfort each other, since Isla grieved for her cousin as well. He also told her Slade had survived, which brought joy to her heart in spite of her grief. According to Tiernay, the boy had caused a diversion to distract the soldiers on the night they escaped the fortress. Then he hid in the forest for several days until finding Tiernay after the battle.

Another letter followed from Tiernay, but he only mentioned the progress in Brannagh and nothing about their relationship for the most part. However, Airell's response had been vague as well. In truth, she no longer knew what do, with so many responsibilities on her shoulders. Could she still return to him in Brannagh and leave her kingdom to be ruled by a regent? As the weeks passed by, Airell's desire to see him again continued to grow until it was almost unbearable.

One day, Gwyn noticed the carved chess pieces on her window ceil. She held the ebony knight in her palm and studied the detailed engravings. "What game is this?"

Airell sighed and forced a smile. "Chess. Prince Tiernay carved the figurines himself. All the pieces move different ways to protect the king."

Her sister's eyes lit up. "Could you teach me?"

She nodded. "Aye, someday, but the game is incomplete. I couldn't fit the board in my bag."

"We could make one! I'm certain Isla would love to learn how to play as well." Airell hesitated, but her sister's unbridled enthusiasm convinced her in the end and she agreed.

A few days later, a woodworker finished crafting a smooth and square wooden slab. Then, Airell and Gwyn carefully painted red and black squares. By the end of the week, the game was complete.

However, as she sat across from her sister and started setting up the board, Airell couldn't go on. She wiped tears from her cheeks and looked up into Gwyn's concerned eyes. "I'm sorry. I promised Tiernay I would keep a chess game waiting for him. Yet, I fear he will never return. There seem to be too many obstacles in our way."

Gwyn gripped her hand from across the table. "My sister, there are no obstacles too big for God. Give it time. You never know what miracles He could do." She paused with a strange look in her eyes Airell had never seen before. "I'm still holding out hope for King Tristan. The letter said his cousin continues searching for him. Perhaps he survived."

Airell squeezed her sister's hand and gave her a knowing smile. "You're right, sister. We will have to keep praying and never give up hope."

CHAPTER THIRTY-THREE

Gazing Upward

King Tiernay approached the gates of Daireann in the midmorning, after a three-week journey. He had been worn out from the long trek through the mountains only moments ago, but now with the knowledge his love awaited him within the castle walls, his strength had been renewed. Several archers and Lord Edmund met his company from the top of the ramparts when they approached the gate. They were intimidating at first, until Airell's uncle recognized him. Then they lowered their arrows and the gates were opened.

When Tiernay walked in with Slade, he was met by Airell's mother, sister and Isla, who seemed surprised to see him and the servant boy.

While Isla and Slade had a joyful reunion, the queen and princess greeted Tiernay warmly.

He took off his leather riding gloves and twisted them nervously in his hands. "May I please speak with Queen Airell? It is of much importance. Have I arrived at an inconvenient time?"

"No," Lady Gwyneth answered. "My sister has been anxious to see you, but I'm afraid she is not in the castle. She has gone to her favorite retreat to think and pray, but she will return shortly."

Tiernay sighed and tried to hide his disappointment. "Oh, I see. Could I trouble you for a room to stay in the castle for a few days until her return? I apologize for coming unannounced."

The queen mother smiled. "Certainly, you are our honored guest, King Tiernay. You are welcome here as long as you like. However, you will not need to wait a few days to speak with my daughter. She is only a short walk away, sitting on the cliff overlooking Loch Maorga."

Airell stared whimsically at the puffy clouds above her, reflecting on the past year. The loch below and the sky above had remained the same—peaceful, quiet and full of life—yet she was the one who had changed.

If her travels and experiences had taught her any-thing, it was that so much more life existed beyond her little refuge on the cliff. It spite of all the hardships in the past year, including the deaths of her father and brother, she had much to be thankful for.

It seemed her life events happened all at once and then paused for a time of reflection. Now she awaited her next adventure. Except, Airell was no longer the naïve young princess she had been a year ago—terrified of the future. She had become responsible for the well-being of many—the heir of King Fallon—Queen of Daireann. While she longed to travel back to Brannagh and be reunited with Tiernay, remembering her people would be affected by the decision kept her grounded.

Tiernay faced the same choice and Airell finally knew the truth—their kingdoms would forever keep them apart.

Airell closed her eyes, concentrating on the soft bed of grass under her head and the warm summer breeze teasing the golden strands of hair surrounding her face. Then she started to pray.

God, it breaks my heart to believe we would fall in love only to be ripped apart from each other. But I trust you. If we are meant to forever travel down separate paths, help me to accept it and learn to be content in your will for my life.

"Airell..." a deep voice called in the distance and then drifted away on the breeze.

She kept her eyes closed, believing it to only be in her imagination. Perhaps she was dreaming again.

"Airell..."

The voice sounded closer this time, but she didn't dare look. If it was a dream, she wanted to remain in it for as long as possible—for if she opened her eyes, he would disappear like so many times before.

"Airell?"

This time the voice seemed to come from directly above her head. She peeked through one eyelid and then opened both, blinking several times in disbelief. There was a young king kneeling above her with a royal blue robe draped over his shoulders. "Tiernay? Is this a dream?"

His hazel eyes gazed into hers as he brushed her cheek with his fingertips. "No, but it feels like it, my love. I am sorry I could not return sooner."

Happy tears filled Airell's eyes, but she remained in a daze. "I kept the game ready for you."

A smile bloomed on his lips. "Good. I'm ready to be beaten again, Milady."

Airell scrambled from her place on the ground, rather ungracefully in her excitement and launched herself into his arms.

He let out a small yelp of surprise while losing his balance. Then they both tumbled backward into the tall grass, laughing in each other's embrace.

"*Airell*," she corrected with a giggle while sitting up beside him and caressing his cheek. "How many times do I have to remind you to call me by my first name? You *are* still my husband after all."

A handsome smile bloomed on his lips as he sat up directly across from her. "*Airell*, it has seemed like an eternity since we parted in Dóchas. I know much has changed, but I came hoping you still feel as we did all those months ago."

She frowned as reality came crashing down around her. "Of course I do, but I cannot leave my people to be forever ruled by a regent."

"Nor I," he agreed. "So what if we made a compromise?"

Airell stared at him in wonder. "I'm afraid I do not understand."

"Soon we will rebuild our ships in Brannagh. We could travel here during the fall and winter seasons to avoid the bitter cold winters. Then we will spend the warmer seasons in my kingdom. We could have the best of both, my love. And most important of all, we could be together."

Airell thought over his proposal for a few moments, never dreaming it would be possible, but finally she looked up and nodded with a happy smile. "There is nothing I would love more."

He pulled her up with him and spun her in a circle as they both laughed. "You've just made me the happiest man in Ardena." He lowered her feet to the ground and gave her a tender kiss before getting down on one knee.

Airell struggled to catch her breath. "What are you doing? We are wed already. Do you not remember?"

He smiled and kissed her hand. "I want to start out our new lives together properly this time. Lady Airell of Daireann, I cannot imagine loving anyone as I love you, nor ruling a kingdom without you as my queen. You have already married me once out of duty to your people. Now will you marry me again because your heart has chosen me?"

"Aye," she whispered and knelt so they were face to face. "You came into my life when I thought all my decisions had been made for me." She paused and ran her fingers over his cheek. "Now I realize God led me to the right choice from the very beginning."

DISCUSSION QUESTIONS

1. Airell's life goes through a dramatic transformation during the story. What did her travels teach her about life? Can you think of an important event in your life that has changed you for the better?

2. At first, Tiernay believes his soul is unredeemable because of the horrible things his uncle has made him do. What characters and events in the story influence him to believe differently and become the king God intends for him to be?

3. Psalm 23 brings Airell great comfort throughout the story. What does this verse mean to you? Do you have a verse that brings you comfort during difficult times?

4. Discuss some of the events and misunderstandings that cause the rift between Tiernay and Tristan. How do they make amends? Would it be difficult for you to forgive after going through something similar? Read what Romans 12:19 says about taking revenge and talk about what it means to you.

5. King Arlan shows great courage while battling his illness. What lessons can his life and death teach us about how to live by faith even when facing difficulty?

For more discussion questions, please visit:
rachelskatvold.com

Ardena

Royal Lineages

Spring, 1187 AD

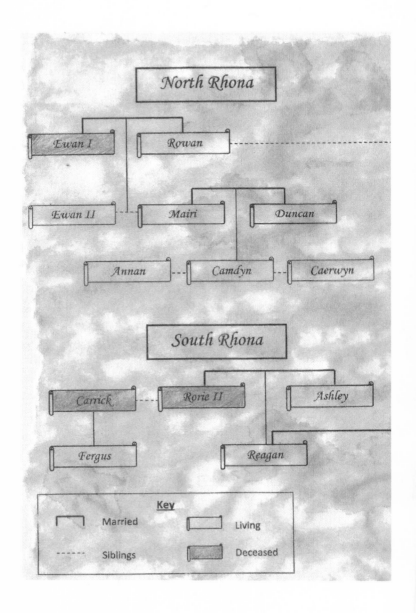

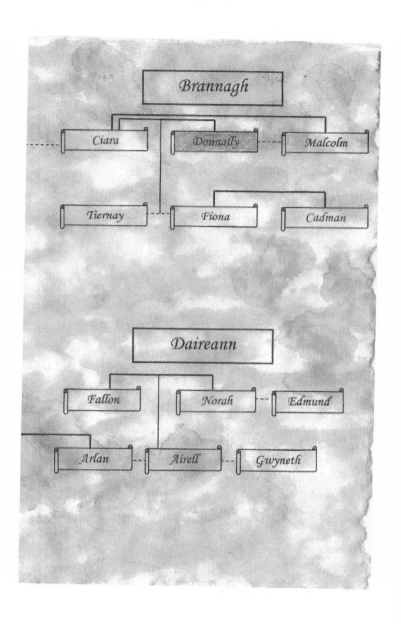

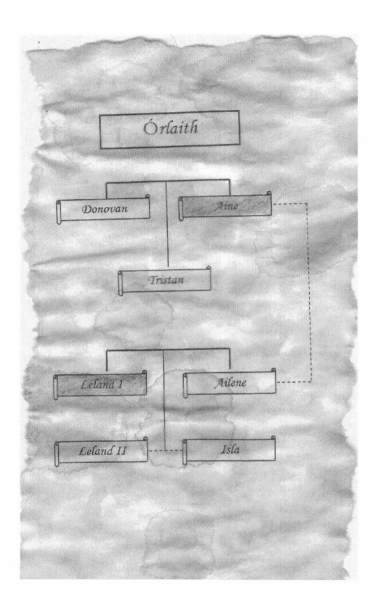

Pronunciations

&

Meanings

Characters in Ladies of Ardena Series
Airell /*air-el*/ of noble birth
Aine /*awn-ya*/ radiance or joy
Ailene /*ay-leen*/ little noble one
Annan /*an-nan*/ from the stream
Arlan /*ar-lin*/ pledge or oath
Artair /*art-tear*/ like a bear
Ashley /*ash-lee*/ lives in the ash tree grove
Cadman /*cad-men*/ warrior
Caerwyn /*care-win*/ white fort
Camdyn /*cam-din*/ enclosed valley
Cearul /kar-ul/ fierce in battle
Ciara /*kee-ra*/ saint
Carrick /*care-ick*/ rock
Clare /*cl-air*/ bright light
Donnally /*don-nelly*/ brown-haired man or chieftain
Donovan /*dawn-uh-vin*/ strong fighter
Doughlas /*dug-liss*/ dwells by the dark stream
Duncan /*dun-kin*/ dark warrior
Edmund /*ed-mun-d*/ fortunate protector
Ewan /*you-in* / youth or God is good
Fallon /*fal-on*/ royalty
Fergus /*fur-gus*/ strong man
Fiona /*fee-ona*/ fair
Gwyneth /*gwen-eth*/ blessed
Isla /*eye-la*/ rocky place or island
Leland /*lee-land*/ fallow land
Liam /*lee-am*/ protector
Mairi /*mah-ree*/ beloved
Merrie /*mear-ee*/ joyful
Malcolm /*mal-cum*/ follower
Norah /*nor-ah*/ honor
Peadar /*pad-ar*/ rock
Reagan /*ray-gan*/ the king's child or impulsive

Rorie /*roar-ee*/ red king
Rowan /*row-in*/ little red headed one
Tiernay / *teer-nay*/ regal
Tristan /*triss-tan*/ tumult or outcry
Slade /*sl-aid*/ child of the valley

Kingdoms and Villages
Áthas /*Ah-ha-s* / joy and gladness
Beatha /*Ba-ha*/ life
Brannagh /*bran-na*/ beauty, dark as a raven
Dóchas /*doe-hass*/ hope
Daireann /*dar-rawn*/ fruitful and bountiful
Kiely /kee-lee / descendants of the graceful one
Órlaith /*or-la*/ golden princess
Rhona: /*row-nah*/ saint or rough island

Other Places
Dorcha Cliffs /*dar-ha* / dark cliffs
Dub Hach Fortress / *doo-ah*/ gloomy fortress
Loch Maorga /*mu-air-gah*/ majestic lake
Óir Mountains /*or*/ gold mountains
Solas Fortress /*su-lus*/ light fortress

Middle English Terms
Sennight: a week
Fortnight: two weeks
Aye: yes
'Tis: a contraction for 'it is'
'Twas: a contraction for 'it was'

EXCERPT FROM:

LADY REAGAN'S QUEST

Prologue

Kingdom of South Rhona, Ardena
Spring, 1175 AD

"Slow down!" Ewan called before sucking in a breath. The chase had been fun at first when he caught the servant girl spying on him through the bushes, but now his legs had grown quite weary and his chest heaved from exertion.

"*Slow down?*" the girl called out with a laugh as the summer breeze whipped through her fiery red curls. "This is a race. 'Tis it not?"

The young prince tried to keep up as she dashed toward a grove of trees in the distance. Her feet were bare, yet she had no trouble navigating the craggy earth at a rapid speed. He had outrun many lads in his kingdom, but he was no match for her. "I merely wish to know your name!"

Another joyous laugh echoed back. "You'll have to catch me first!"

Soon they reached the trees and the girl paused for a moment as she eyed the branches above. Then in one swift movement, she grabbed onto the lowest branch of one of the trees and swung her body upward, revealing she wore boy's trousers under her gown. Once firmly situated on the branch, she climbed up to the next one and then stood, bracing herself against the trunk with one hand as a proud grin spread across her freckled face. "Now I know you can run, but can you climb?"

Ewan braced his hands on his thighs for a moment to catch his breath. Then he looked back up and shook his head in wonder. The servant girl had to be half squirrel. Was it worth the effort to continue his pursuit? Right this moment he was supposed to be meeting his future betrothed—South Rhona's young queen—but instead he had taken off for a spontaneous game of chase with a half-feral servant girl. He would most likely be chastised severely for his behavior when he returned to the castle, however, a moment later he found himself shinnying up the tree after her. What would a few more minutes hurt, if he was already in trouble?

A few minutes into his clumsy pursuit, the prince finally caught up with the servant girl at the top of the tree and braced his body against an adjacent branch while sucking in a few ragged breaths.

When he looked over at the girl, she grinned and swiped her brow with the back of her sleeve, smearing the streaks of dirt further across her face. She appeared to be around twelve years old—only a couple years younger than him. "You passed my test. You have proved a worthy opponent, Your Highness."

"Aye," Ewan rasped before clearing his throat.

"Now will you tell me your name?"

"I supposed you have earned it." Her grin widened as she swept an auburn ringlet from her forehead and gave a slight bow while taking care to keep her balance. "Lady Reagan, at your service."

Ewan's face paled. "*Queen* Reagan?"

"Aye and you are *Prince* Ewan, are you not?"

He stared at her in disbelief. "You knew who I was the entire time?"

A mischievous grin bloomed on her lips. "Why do you think I ran? I had planned to hide the entire afternoon, but you caught me."

Ewan threw his head back and laughed at her bold confession. "I must say, I have never met anyone as strange or interesting as you, Milady."

Her emerald eyes twinkled. "I'll take that as a compliment."

They shared another laugh, but a loud cracking sound interrupted. Ewan felt the branch he rested on give way and his gaze locked with Reagan's, whose eyes were now filled with terror.

"Ewan!" she shouted and lurched forward with an outstretched hand.

He reached with all his might, but it was all for naught. His fingers barely brushed hers before the branch snapped in half, sending him crashing through a tangle of branches. They slapped, scraped and gouged his body all the way down. Then the side of his head struck a large knot on the lowest branch before he landed on the forest floor with a hollow thump. Ewan stared toward the sky as Reagan scrambled down the tree, screaming and trying to reach him. Her tear-streaked face and concerned emerald eyes appeared above him, framed by a tangle of red curls a few moments before his vision faded to black.

"Foolish girl!" Reagan's mother reprimanded while scouring her shelves for bandages and medicines. "We are trying to make an alliance with North Rhona. Maiming their prince is not the right way to make peace."

Reagan avoided her mother's eyes. Instead, she peered down at the raven-haired prince and gently lifted the blood-soaked bandage she held on the laceration near his temple. The bleeding had slowed a little, but he would most likely have a scar for the rest of his life—if he lived. His other injuries were much worse, including a broken leg and a few cracked ribs. However, she knew from experience after helping her mother in the infirmary, internal bleeding was also a concern. It was her fault.

Her mother returned with supplies and the aroma of alcohol stung Reagan's nostrils as she cleaned the wound and then stitched it closed. "And why are you dressed like a servant?"

Reagan delayed answering for a moment while wrapping a clean bandage around Ewan's head, careful to be gentle. Then she stifled a sob. "I'm sorry, Mother. I only wanted to meet my future betrothed in privacy, without the entire kingdom watching us."

"You have received your wish, Daughter," the queen mother muttered while walking toward the foot of the bed to check on the prince's other injuries. "However, if the King and Queen of North Rhona see their son in this condition, I'm afraid the alliance agreement will end abruptly. "Come, help me clean him up and splint the leg. We must make haste before they return from their walk in the gardens with your uncle."

Reagan wiped her tears on the back of her sleeve and nodded. Within half an hour, they had washed the caked blood off the prince's wounds, splinted his leg and bound his ribs. He looked much better than before, but still hadn't woken up. She knew it wasn't a good sign.

Commotion erupted outside the door and her mother's eyes grew wide as she turned to Reagan. "That will be the King and Queen. Stay here." She handed her a cup of powdered herbs mixed with water. "If he wakes up, give him this to drink. He will be in a great amount of pain."

Reagan nodded before watching her mother leave and close the door quickly behind her. Then, alone with the prince, she held his hand and smoothed back his dark shoulder-length hair. "I'm sorry," she whispered while fighting more tears. "This is my fault." Reagan leaned in close to his ear. "Please live. Ewan…please wake up." She sniffled and closed her eyes before kissing his cheek. "I'm so sorry."

Hearing movement, Reagan's eyes flew open and saw the prince blink once and then twice. He tried to lift his head, but grimaced with the movement.

Reagan placed her hand on his shoulder "Please try to relax, Milord. You've been badly injured."

When Ewan's eyes focused on her, his body relaxed and he took in a few ragged breaths. "You're here."

Reagan smiled through her tears. "Aye, although I'm certain you wish to never set eyes on my face again."

"Quite the contrary, Milady. To be awakened by a kiss is well worth the pain of falling." He released a light chuckle and then groaned, holding his ribs.

She reached for the cup of medicine her mother

had prepared. "Here, you need to drink this. 'Twill help with the pain." Reagan lifted his head and held the cup to his lips for him to take a sip. Then she helped him rest back against his pillow. "I venture you did not expect our betrothal going this way." She paused and wiped away a rogue tear. "I'm so sorry. My wild spirit causes nothing but trouble. I must ask your forgiveness, Milord."

Ewan winced and drew in a few ragged breaths before managing a frail smile. "Kiss me again and I'll consider it."

Reagan blushed at his bold statement, but guessed he wasn't in his right mind because of his head injury. Still, she couldn't deny her own heart either. Reagan leaned her face toward his and closed her eyes.

A moment later, the King and Queen came bursting through the door, exclaiming over Ewan's injuries and the fact they had been lied to.

Reagan leapt off the stool and escaped the room to avoid their wrath. In the hallway, she came face to face with her mother. "Have I ruined the alliance?"

Her mother's lips formed a straight line while she placed her hands on Reagan's shoulders, but then her expression softened. "I do not know, daughter. Only time will tell. If this alliance fails, we will accept the one with Daireann."

Reagan shuttered at the thought of moving away from her homeland. At least with their alliance with North Rhona she could stay closer to her mother. Now everything had been ruined because of her.

The door swung open and the new North Rhonan king emerged with his son cradled in his muscular arms, jaw clenched and angry tears in his eyes.

The king's large stature and war braids scattered

through his raven hair would have intimidated most people, but Reagan's mother rushed forward anyway. "Oh, you should not be moving him! I'm begging you, Milord."

"We are taking him home where he belongs," the man growled. "Now move out of my way."

Lady Ashley didn't give in and blocked the hallway. "'Tis unlikely he will survive the trip with his injuries. Please, allow him time to recover. I will care for him myself."

Ewan's mother was not far behind, eyes blazing. "You have done enough, Lady Ashley! We should have known something like this would happen. Our kingdoms will never have peace because your people will never understand our way of life. You only make excuses and empty promises." With that said, the king and queen shouldered their way past her mother.

Reagan struggled to breathe, watching the young prince drift away from her. Before they turned the corner, Ewan's eyes met hers and he managed a pained smile in her direction. She wiped her tears and smiled back, hoping to give him strength and the will to survive the long journey home.

Even if they never set eyes on each other again—even if their kingdoms would remain enemies—Reagan would never forget the North Rhonan prince. In the short time they spent together, he had stolen a piece of her heart—a piece she didn't want returned.

Books by Rachel Skatvold

Ladies of Ardena

Lady Airell's Choice
Lady Reagan's Quest
Coming 2019

Whispers in Wyoming

Guardian of her Heart
A Forgetful Heart
Melodies of the Heart

Hart Ranch Series

Escaping Reality
Chasing Embers

Riley Family Legacy Novellas

Beauty Within
Beauty Unveiled
Beauty Restored

About the Author

Rachel Skatvold is a Christian author and stay-at-home mom from the Midwest. She enjoys writing inspirational romance and encouraging blogs. Rachel completed her first series, the Riley Family Legacy Novellas in 2014 and is now working on the Hart Ranch Series, set in the Montana wilderness and the Ladies of Ardena Series, set in medieval times. She is also a contributing author in the Whispers in Wyoming Series. Other than writing, some of her hobbies include singing, reading and camping in the great outdoors with her husband and two young sons. You can find more information about Rachel and her books on her website: www.rachelskatvold.com.